THE GOLDEN HORSEMEN OF BAGHDAD

THE GOLDEN HORSEMEN OF BAGHDAD

SAVIOUR PIROTTA

BLOOMSBURY EDUCATION
LONDON OXFORD NEW YORK NEW DELHI SYDNEY

BLOOMSBURY EDUCATION
Bloomsbury Publishing Plc
50 Bedford Square, London, WC1B 3DP, UK

BLOOMSBURY, BLOOMSBURY EDUCATION and the Diana logo are trademarks of
Bloomsbury Publishing Plc

First published in Great Britain 2019 by Bloomsbury Publishing Plc

A catalogue record for this book is available from the British Library

ISBN: PB: 978-1-4729-5599-9; ePDF: 978-1-4729-5598-2; ePub: 978-1-4729-5597-5

2 4 6 8 10 9 7 5 3 1

Typeset by Newgen KnowledgeWorks Pvt. Ltd., Chennai, India
Printed and bound by CPI Group (UK) Ltd, Croydon, CR04YY

To find out more about our authors and books visit www.bloomsbury.com
and sign up for our newsletters

For all my readers, children, teaching staff and librarians in the cities of Bradford and Leeds. Thanks for all your support over the years. I wouldn't be here without you.

CONTENTS

CHAPTER ONE

An Unwelcome Visitor

A village outside the city of Baghdad, 798 CE

Jabir ibn Abdel woke up with a start. He'd fallen asleep in his fishing boat again. It was almost dawn. The holy man in the mosque across the river was calling the faithful to prayer.

The moon hung low above the horizon, and all around it the pale sky was still spangled with stars. A stiff breezed rippled the surface of the water. It was going to be a glorious day, sunny but cool. Jabir had planned to meet up with friends in the afternoon. One of them was a champion at wrestling and he was going to show Jabir some new moves. They'd follow that with a game or two of chess before Jabir headed home for dinner. But first he had to haul in his net. 'No work, no play' had been one of his father's favourite sayings and Jabir agreed with him wholeheartedly. You couldn't expect to have fun if you didn't work first. It was the natural order of things.

He washed himself over the side of the boat, noisily rinsing out his nose and ears and raking his fingers through his wet hair. Once clean, he spread out his prayer mat and chanted his morning prayers.

By the time he'd finished, the moon and stars had faded. On the banks of the river, geese honked and toads croaked in the tall papyrus reeds. Jabir hauled in his fishing net. It felt light in his hand and he knew even before it surfaced that it was virtually empty.

Jabir shook his head at the few anchovies flopping around the deck, gasping for water. Poor fish, he thought, they'd blundered upriver from the open sea only to be caught in a fisherman's net. He scooped them up gently in his hands and returned them to the water.

'Hurry back to the ocean,' he said as the fish darted away for safety. 'And make sure you grow up big and strong, then no one will catch you.'

Jabir had to admit that he was no good at fishing. His heart just wasn't in it. His father had been one of the most respected fishermen on the Tigris. No one could net a carp or a shoal of catfish as quickly or as deftly as Abdel al-Kabir. He'd tried to teach Jabir his trade, just as his own father had done before him. But Jabir simply couldn't get the hang of it. No matter how hard he tried, his mind always wandered and he ended up daydreaming about something or other, or he indulged in his hobby of whittling. He'd carved a lot of useful things on the boat: knife handles, whistles, even cups and bowls. He made little wooden toys too, animals mostly, which his sisters played with in the dust outside their house. But his nets always came out of the water empty.

But now that his father had gone to an early grave, Jabir was left to provide for his mother and three sisters on his own.

It wasn't fair, he thought. Twelve-year-old boys shouldn't have to look after an entire family. If only he had an uncle or a grandparent to help him financially, or at least give him advice. But his father had no brothers. He had been an only child and his own parents had died even before Jabir was born. And Jabir's mother's family were desert people. Jabir had never even met them. Apparently, even getting a message to them when they were travelling with their camels was difficult.

Still, Jabir thought, it was no use complaining. There were lots of children in the same situation. Life was dangerous but you had to look it straight in the face and fight back, at least with your mind, if not with physical strength.

Jabir rowed ashore and strung his fishing net along a rubble wall to dry. He tried not to look at the other fishermen who were transferring heaps of glittering fish from their boats to large wicker baskets. His face burned with shame. All his big thoughts on the river evaporated and he dreaded going back home empty-handed. What was he going to tell his mother? 'Sorry, *umi*! There's nothing to eat again today! You might as well put out the fire and save the kindling.'

No, he couldn't go back home without something to show for his night on the river. By hook or by crook, he had to get hold of some fish. Jabir ran his hands through his thick curly hair, thinking – and that gave him a brilliant idea.

An hour or so later he stepped into his mother's kitchen with a triumphant grin on his face, and a large carp dangling from a hook in his right hand.

'You have been lucky today, *abnay*!' exclaimed his mother. 'That carp is big enough to feed all of us for at least three days. You'll be as good a fisherman as your father soon.'

Jabir's sister, Ayat, looked up from the mortar where she was grinding spices. 'You've been to the barber's on the way home, Jabir?'

Her brother rubbed his newly shaved head, hoping against hope his guilt wouldn't show in his face. 'My hair was getting too long. It kept getting in my eyes while I was fishing.'

He wondered if Ayat had guessed he'd sold his hair to a wig-maker so he could buy the carp. If so, she didn't let on. She held up hands stained bright yellow with spice. 'Let me put that fish in cold water. *Umi* and I will stuff it with herbs before we roast it.'

'Where are the twins?' asked Jabir.

'They're picking mint in the meadow,' replied Ayat.

'Don't let them stay out too long,' said Jabir, remembering what his father used to tell his mother about him when he was little. 'It's going to be really hot today.' He filled a basin with water to wash his face. 'I'm going out with my friends now, but I'll be home in time for supper.'

*   *   *

They ate the evening meal under the ancient fig tree outside the house, sitting cross-legged in the dust. There were five of them: Mother, Jabir, Ayat, and the young twins, Nadya and Zubayda.

The carp, stuffed with herbs, spices and pine nuts and roasted slowly in the embers of an outdoor fire, tasted delicious and they all licked their fingers.

'Well done, *umi* and Ayat,' said Jabir, touching his stomach as he burped loudly, to show he'd enjoyed the food. 'Another fine feast to be remembered.'

'And we must thank you for catching such a big fish,' replied his mother, which made Jabir's face burn with shame for lying.

'Have you finished the lion you were carving for me, Jabir?' asked Nadya, burping loudly too.

'I'll do it tonight on the boat,' promised Jabir. He patted his pocket where he kept the half-finished toy.

'And when you've finished Nadya's lion, you can make me a camel,' said Zubayda.

The twins loved the animals Jabir carved. They were the best toys in the village and children from neighbouring houses often came over to play with them.

'Story time,' said Mother, hanging a coloured glass lamp in the branches of the fig tree, where it winked like a magical star.

Ayat brought out a basket of nectarines to share during the storytelling. She was a gifted storyteller, using different voices for the characters in her tales. Even Jabir, who considered himself too old to enjoy stories, got drawn in, gasping as loudly as the twins at the clever twists in the plot.

Tonight's story was called 'The Fisherman and the Djinn', and Ayat had just come to the exciting bit where the fisherman persuades the genie to squeeze into a small glass bottle, when a horse cantered down the alleyway. It stopped by the fig tree and pawed at the dust with one of its hoofs. Sitting straight-backed in the saddle was a gaunt man with a long beard and a black turban.

It was Yusuf Said, the landlord, a rich man who owned half the village, including the little tumbledown house where Jabir and his family lived.

'Good evening,' he said, touching his turban as a sign of respect to Jabir's mother but without getting off his horse. A small jewelled amulet glittered at his throat and gold teeth flashed in his mouth.

Jabir scrambled to his feet while his mother quickly drew her veil across her face. '*Marhaba*, sir! Ayat, fetch the landlord a glass of mint tea.'

The landlord held up one hand. 'Don't bother about the tea. I'm not stopping.'

He looked directly at Jabir, recognising him as the head of the household. A frosty smile appeared on his lips. It reminded Jabir of a snake about to pounce on a helpless mouse. 'You are late with your rent.'

'I'm sorry,' replied Jabir. 'We buried my father less than a moon ago and money has been difficult to come by. But we'll have it for you soon.'

The landlord touched his chest respectfully at the mention of Abdel's death but his eyes remained steely. 'I am sorry for your loss. But I expect to be paid on time. With your father gone, I fear you will not be able to find the money.'

Jabir's mother stepped forward. 'My son has inherited his father's boat and fishing net. He is now a fisherman in his own right. Why, only today he caught a carp big enough to feed the whole family for days. Soon he'll be catching enough fish to sell.'

'From what I hear around the village, your son has not inherited his father's gift with the fishing net,' sneered the landlord. He turned to Jabir. 'You were lucky today on the river, eh?'

Zubayda piped up bravely from her mother's side. 'The carp was delicious. People will pay good money for tasty fish like that.'

The landlord laughed. 'Will they?'

He stared at Jabir's newly shaved head, and for a horrific moment Jabir thought he was going to shame him in front of his mother. He'd obviously been making enquiries about him in the village. How else would he know that Jabir was useless at fishing? Had he found out that Jabir had sold his hair to buy the carp too?

But if the landlord knew about it, he wasn't telling. Instead he reached inside his saddlebag and drew out a rolled parchment. 'This is a formal document drawn up by my notary in Baghdad. You have until the full moon to pay all your arrears and next month's rent. If you fail to settle the debt with me, I will have you evicted from your home.'

'Until the full moon?' gasped Jabir's mother, tightening the veil around her mouth. 'That is not long enough.'

The landlord flung the rolled-up parchment at Jabir's feet. 'I have good tenants waiting for this property should you be forced to leave. Have the money ready.'

The horse whinnied as he tugged on the reins, ready to go. The landlord drew out a sword and smashed the coloured lamp. Bits of broken glass rained down on the twins, who screamed in fear and stepped away from the fig tree.

The landlord laughed. 'Remember, you have until the full moon to pay me.'

'Why is he so horrible?' asked Ayat as the landlord's horse cantered back down the alley.

'Even as a boy, he was always cruel,' replied her mother.

'You knew the landlord when you were children?' said Jabir.

But his mother would not say anything else about the matter. 'Pick up the broken glass before you come in,' she said.

* * *

It was late at night. Jabir closed the door gently behind him and hurried down the road. The muezzin had long called the *Salat al-Isha*, the last prayer of the day, and the only sound in the village was snoring coming out of open windows.

Jabir walked with a fierce determination. One way or another, he was determined to start catching fish. Baskets full of them! He'd earn enough to pay off the family's debts *and* meet their future rent. He'd even earn enough to buy a few egg-laying hens. That would be another source of income. His mother and sisters need never worry about keeping a roof over their heads again.

By the time he reached the riverbank, the moon was already high in the sky and the only boats still moored belonged to the boys he'd spent the afternoon with. The rest had sailed out to the fishing grounds already. Jabir stopped by the wall where he'd left his net to dry, and his heart missed a beat. The net was gone.

'Your landlord took it earlier this evening,' said one of his friends, who was filling a clay jar with live bait. His name was Ali. 'We tried to stop him but he brought guards with him, the dirty coward. He said it was his right to take the net; it would help pay for the rent you owe.'

Jabir felt the blood rise to his head. His face felt all hot and his eyes smarted. 'That son of a jackal will not stop me from fishing. Will one of you lend me a spare net?'

'We would,' said Ali, 'but I'm afraid it won't be any use. The landlord also took your boat. His guards lifted it right out of the water and hauled it on to a donkey cart. You can come fishing with me, if you like, though. I'll pay you.'

Jabir shook his head. 'That's very kind of you, Ali, but I wouldn't be any help. I'm too angry to work properly.'

He watched in silence as his friends sailed out on to the river, the sails on the larger boats fluttering in the breeze like the wings of doves. His mind whirled. Why would the landlord take away his only means of livelihood if he wanted him to pay his debts? It made no sense. And then, in a flash, Jabir had it. The landlord did not want him to pay the rent. He wanted to throw him and his family out. He must have plans for the house. Maybe he would do it up and rent it to a richer tenant.

But Jabir wasn't going to let him. He would find another way to pay his debts. He was no good at fishing, true. But this was a blessing in disguise, as the imam would no doubt tell him. All obstacles are hurdles, waiting for you to jump over them.

Jabir turned away from the river. He would find something else to do for a living, something he actually enjoyed doing. He would win in the end, because as the old proverb says, 'Oil always floats on water and good triumphs over evil.'

CHAPTER TWO

Trouble in the Merchant's House

Jabir trudged along the dusty road to Baghdad, his one spare robe parceled up tightly under his left arm. It was not yet midday but the heat was unbearable. Away from the river, the air was dry and dusty. Jabir's throat felt like it was lined with ground glass. There was a wind blowing up, which raked his face with grit.

Jabir walked faster. He wanted to get to Baghdad by sundown and hopefully find somewhere to spend the night before the muezzin called the last prayers of the day.

Out of habit, he tried remembering if he'd moored his boat securely enough to withstand a stiff wind. Then he remembered – he didn't have a fishing boat any more. Yusuf Said had stolen it. Even thinking about it made his blood boil.

'Do not waste your feelings on a crook like him, *abnay*,' his mother had said when he broke the news. 'Think of what you're going to do next. We might be penniless, but you have youth and strength on your side.'

'I'll go to Baghdad and find work,' said Jabir. 'It's the busiest city in the world. Someone will give me a job.'

'But what will you do there?' asked Zubayda.

'I have no idea,' replied Jabir, 'but believe me, I'll find a way to make us rich.'

'Well said,' cried his mother. 'A magnificent tree always starts with a humble little seed.'

And so Jabir had left Ayat in charge of the family and set off to Baghdad at dawn. The city was the centre of the Islamic world. If he couldn't earn money from fishing, he'd earn it there. The imam in the village had told him that nearly a million people lived in Baghdad. Some of them were so rich, it was said that the caliph's wife ate out of dishes made of gold and silver and studded with precious stones. The city was home to famous scholars, inventors, doctors, poets, authors and all manner of scientists. Surely someone there would give him a job?

As he walked, Jabir wondered what kind of work he'd be able to get. He'd never learned to read or write and he had no tools except his humble whittling knife should any craftsman offer him an apprenticeship. Perhaps he could be a messenger, running errands for busy merchants and shopkeepers. He'd heard there were a lot of bookshops in Baghdad. Even if he couldn't read, he might be able to get a job in one of them, perhaps cleaning and tidying up. Or he could try for a post with a baker. His father, who'd been to Baghdad twice in his lifetime, claimed no one in the world made finer cakes and sweetmeats than Baghdadi bakers. They charged a lot of money for their famous creations, which they baked with spices from faraway lands. Perhaps he could train to be a master baker. He would not only send money home, but also cakes in special boxes with his name written on them.

*   *   *

Late in the afternoon, the sky turned an alarming shade of yellow. A sandstorm was on the way. Jabir walked faster. If there was going to be a sandstorm, he didn't want to get caught in it. People were known to go blind in sandstorms, their eyeballs raked to shreds with flying grit.

By now he could see the walls of Baghdad looming up ahead. He broke into a run and approached a gate where hundreds of people were trying to get in. The guards had given up trying to keep order and were desperately trying to push the gate shut before the storm broke.

Jabir forced his way through the crowd, like a crab dragging itself through river slush. Slowly he got to the front where a group of older men in pristine white robes were hammering on the iron gate with their fists.

'Let us in! You can't leave us out here to die.'

'There's a woman with us.'

Jabir turned to see four men in red tunics and sashes carrying a litter with velvet curtains. The city gate was pulled open at once – it was actually two gates, one right behind the other. The men in tunics hefted the litter through and the rest of the crowd poured in behind it before the guards could close the gates again.

Within minutes, the entire crowd seemed to vanish as if by djinn's magic. Everyone had somewhere to go for shelter, Jabir thought, as he looked at the last of the men disappearing down a narrow side street. He was standing on a straight, wide avenue. There were large, brightly painted houses on either side, with tall date palms rising up behind the walls. At the far end, the golden dome of a mosque glittered in the eerie light. The trees shook in the wind. Every single door and window seemed to be firmly shut.

The storm hit without warning, sweeping Jabir off his feet and hurling him across the street as if he were a rag doll. He crashed into a wall and howled with pain. The street around him became a dizzying blur as whirling sand obscured the buildings and the streets. Unfurling his spare robe, Jabir managed to twist it into a thick rope. He wound it tightly round his head, leaving just a narrow gap for his eyes.

He managed to drag himself along the pavement and find shelter in a doorway. He banged on the door with both fists.

'Is anyone there? Let me in, please. I'm going to die out here.'

If anyone heard him, they did not answer.

Jabir crawled on his hands and knees to the next house. Once again, no one replied. He continued down the street, but now the wind was so fierce he could hardly move. At last he found a gate that flew open when he rattled the knocker. He crawled into a tiled courtyard with lanterns swinging wildly in the wind. He managed to force the gate shut behind him and sat with his back to it, gasping for breath in its shelter.

'Hello? *Marhaba?*' he shouted into the wind but, yet again, there was no answer. Instead, a piercing shriek made him jump. Jabir looked round to see a peacock hunched behind the base of a fountain. It fixed him with a beady, angry eye, as if he was responsible for the storm. Behind it, he could make out a second door. It was painted sky-blue. Slowly he crawled past the peacock towards it. The door opened when he turned the handle and Jabir found himself in a silent room. The warmth of a fire and the delicious smell of cooking meat wrapped themselves around him.

'*Marhaba?*' he tried calling again, but the sand in his throat made him wheeze. No one came. Jabir unwrapped the gown from around his head and sat still. His eyes itched horribly but he knew it was dangerous to rub them. The sand would scratch his eyeballs. Instead he blinked rapidly, forcing tears to run down his face. They carried the sand with them until his eyes stopped itching. Now that he could see, Jabir spied a large jug

29

on a counter. Quickly, he poured water into his hands and rinsed his face.

Jabir looked around the room. It was a kitchen bigger than his entire house. The walls were covered in tiles with geometric patterns and there were narrow windows of coloured glass.

Enormous joints of meat and bunches of drying herbs hung from the ceiling, along with an array of iron pots and pans. Dishes of ripe fruit and bowls of yoghurt sat in rows on a marble counter. The conical lid of a steaming tagine rattled away on the fire.

The wonderful aroma of the stew was overpowering. Jabir's stomach rumbled loudly. He hadn't eaten anything since leaving home and he suddenly realised how ravenous he was. He watched, hypnotised, as sauce overflowed and dribbled down the side of the tagine.

The sound of a guitara carried in from somewhere in the house, along with the murmur of people chatting. A party seemed to be in progress.

Jabir's stomach rumbled noisily again and he crept closer to the tagine. Surely no one would mind or even notice if he took just a drop, a tiny lick of stew...

His hand trembling with anticipation, Jabir reached out and scooped up the sauce running down the side of the pot. He was about to put his finger in his mouth when a high-pitched voice made him jump.

'Stop, thief!'

Jabir whirled round on his heels to see an enormously fat man with an elaborate moustache. He was brandishing a kebab skewer. Behind him, several mean-looking fellows streamed into the kitchen through an arched doorway.

They must be the house guards, Jabir thought with a sinking feeling.

'I... I wasn't stealing,' he protested. 'Honestly, I was just wiping the outside of the tagine.'

Jabir's excuses were ignored. The guards grabbed him roughly and, twisting his arms behind his back, forced him through the arched doorway and down a corridor towards a muslin curtain.

Jabir struggled to free himself but the guards were too strong. The muslin curtain was pulled aside and he was dragged into a large hall. It was like being shoved head first into a casket of flashing jewels. The room vibrated with hundreds of bright colours. Tapestries with elaborate patterns hung on the walls. Candles twinkled in glass lamps. The floor was covered in costly rugs and spangled cushions that caught the light. Reclining on them was a small crowd of richly dressed men, most of them sporting flowing beards to show how wealthy they were. Slaves were serving steaming hot food from copper bowls, while musicians played at the end of the room.

The music ground to a halt as the guards pulled Jabir towards a group of men at the other end of the hall from the orchestra.

'We caught a thief in the kitchen, Master Mousa ibn Adam,' declared the cook, his belly quivering with indignation. He pointed at Jabir with the skewer.

An older man with a peacock feather in his turban looked up from his food. 'Put that away before you take out someone's eye,' he snapped at the cook.

'Yes, master. Forgive my ignorance, master.' The cook lowered the skewer while everyone in the hall fell silent. Jabir realised the man with the peacock feather must be the owner of the house, and the host of the party. He was very old, with eyelids that drooped heavily and a moustache that trembled as he spoke.

'Was the back gate not locked?'

'It was, master,' mumbled the cook.

'No it wasn't, sir,' protested Jabir. 'I was seeking shelter from the storm and it opened the moment I rattled the knocker. The kitchen door was open too. I assure you, sir, I did not break in.'

The cook stepped forward. 'Even if the door was open, he will not deny I caught the rascal dipping his hand in the cooking pot, *sayyid*.'

'All right,' said Jabir. 'Perhaps I did give in to temptation, but I didn't have my hand in the pot as you say. I only took the sauce dribbling down the side.' He looked fiercely at the man with the peacock feather. 'I was ravenous, sir, and nearly faint from walking since dawn without a bite to eat. Surely, you wouldn't punish a poor boy for helping himself to a drop of sauce? It would have dribbled on to the burning stove and dried up anyway.'

Mousa turned to his guests, who had all stopped eating and were looking at him intently. 'Gentlemen, we have a conundrum before us. Here is a boy who has stolen food from my kitchen. The law says that he should be punished severely. Yet our religion says that we must be kind and generous to those less fortunate than ourselves. So what should we do? Let him go, or haul him up in front of a judge?'

The rest of the men called out their answers.

'A crime is a crime whatever the reason for it. He should be punished.'

'Let him get away with taking a mouthful of sauce today and he'll be back tomorrow to steal the entire contents of your larder.'

One of the guests leaned closer to a nearby lamp and Jabir's heart froze. It was Yusuf Said, the landlord. 'The boy is a born thief, Mousa. He is a tenant of mine. I know him well.'

'I never stole from the landlord, sir,' protested Jabir. 'In fact, he stole from me. He took my boat and my fishing net.'

'My heart tells me to let the boy go free,' sighed Mousa. 'You can tell by his clothes that he is dirt poor. But I am only a foolish merchant who deals in musical instruments and is prone to bouts of sentimentality. I shall take my guests' advice. Lock the boy in the cellar until we can take him to the judge.'

He nodded at the orchestra. 'More music, please.'

The guards, who had stood back from Jabir as he talked to their master, pounced on him again and dragged him back up the narrow corridor. The sound of music was cut off as a heavy wooden door crashed shut behind him. Jabir stood in the dark, trying very hard not to cry.

It seemed that bad luck had followed him to Baghdad. How was he going to help his mother and sisters now that he would probably end up in jail? How that criminal Yusuf Said must be laughing, Jabir thought bitterly.

But he would have the last laugh. He'd find a way to break free and prove to everyone he was an honest boy, and a breadwinner to boot.

CHAPTER THREE

Prison, and a Prayer!

The sandstorm vanished almost as quickly as it had appeared. The wind dropped, dumping a thick covering of sand that lay like a winter blanket over the entire city. The pavements, the buildings, even the trees seemed to be covered in bright yellow grit.

Jabir could taste it on his lips as Mousa's guards marched him down the street to the judge's house. The cook, dressed in a fine robe but still wearing his chef's hat hurried behind the group, trying to keep up.

Jabir was expecting the judge's house to be a forbidding building with barred windows and guards standing outside brick-built towers. Instead he was hauled into a villa almost as sumptuous as Mousa's. The judge, a young man with brilliantly blue eyes and a well groomed beard, sat cross-legged under a tent in a courtyard. He was reading a thick book with a leather cover.

If the wind had dropped sand in this place, the judge's servants had cleaned it away very quickly. The mosaic floor sparkled and water tinkled in a fountain nearby. Birds swooped and twittered in a cage as big as a fisherman's house. The smell of frying pastry and cinnamon hung in the air.

The judge carefully placed a bookmark between the pages of the book before closing it. He looked Jabir straight in the eye but did not speak to him directly.

'What is the boy's crime?'

'He broke into the house of Mousa ibn Adam, the music merchant, to steal food.'

'I didn't break in,' began Jabir. 'The door was unlocked.'

The judge silenced him with a wave of his hand.

'Was he caught in the act?'

The cook spoke up. 'Yes, sir. I saw him myself. As did the others here with me.'

The judge looked at the guards. 'Is this true?'

'Yes, sir.'

'I only took a drop of stew that was running down the side of a tagine,' argued Jabir. 'And I didn't even get to taste it.'

'But the intention was there,' growled the judge through his ever-present smile. 'A thief is a thief whether he steals a diamond or a cucumber. I find the boy guilty. Take him to prison.'

'That's not fair!' cried Jabir as the guards started dragging him away. 'My mother and my sisters need me. I demand proper justice.'

The judge ignored him and re-opened his book.

'I said "I demand proper justice",' repeated Jabir in a louder voice.

'Have some respect for the law,' snapped one of the guards. 'You should never shout at a judge.'

'Sir,' said the cook, stepping up to the tent, 'how long shall I tell the guards that the boy must stay in prison?'

The judge traced a finger thoughtfully along the calligraphy in the book. 'A month for the crime of breaking and entering. And another month for his disrespect to the law. Now, get him out of my house before he speaks again and I'll be forced to give him three months.'

*   *   *

Jabir's mind reeled. Two whole months in prison. His family would be evicted by the time he was released. Where would they go? He thought about sending them a note but he couldn't write and he had no money to pay for a scribe. Assuming that scribes were allowed to write letters for prisoners. And if they were, and he could afford to pay one for a note, what would he say? That he'd been caught stealing? That would be an even bigger shame for the family than admitting he'd paid for the carp. No, he couldn't send a message to his family.

There was only one thing for it, Jabir decided, as he lay on a mound of straw in his cell. He would do a 'prayer for asking'. He would not pray to be released but for help in rescuing his mother and sisters.

* * *

A day and a half passed and nothing happened. It seemed that Jabir's prayers were not to be answered, but he didn't give up hope. His father had often told him that it took time for prayers to be heard. And then, just after lunch, the door to his cell was thrown open. An old man stood in the doorway with one of the prison guards.

'That's him,' he said, wagging a gnarled finger at Jabir.

Jabir, who'd been sitting on the floor, scrambled to his feet. Why was the old man pointing at him?

Was he in more trouble? He'd done nothing since he'd arrived in prison except pray and sit quietly. Surely they couldn't punish him for that. The old man stepped into the room. He wore a loose tunic that came down to his knees. It was made of a beautiful shiny material, blue with a yellow pattern. Under it a pair of loose pants gleamed clean as mountain snow. Jabir had a feeling he'd seen him somewhere before.

'Don't be alarmed,' said the old man. 'I come in friendship.' He took Jabir's trembling hands in his. 'I was at Mousa's banquet when you were arrested and I couldn't help notice as you were dragged into the room that you have long, elegant fingers. Are you an artist by any chance?'

'I was a fisherman,' replied Jabir. 'but I gave it up because I wasn't any good. I'm trying to find another job, something I can do properly.'

'You have the hands of an artist,' murmured the old man. 'You must not ruin them by harsh work. Do you paint in your spare time? Calligraphy perhaps, or Persian patterns?'

'Sometimes I whittle small wooden toys for my younger sisters,' said Jabir.

'And are you better at whittling than fishing?' asked the gentleman.

'My sisters like the toys I make them, sir.' Jabir searched in his pockets and pulled out the unfinished lion he had been carving for Nadya.

The man took it from him and signalled for the prison guard to bring a lantern. 'This is very good work,' he said, turning the animal over slowly in his hands. 'Are you sure you made it yourself? You didn't steal it?'

'I assure you I made it myself,' replied Jabir, trying very hard to keep the anger out of his voice. Why did people keep doubting his every word? 'I learned how to carve by watching whittlers at the souk in my village, but I seemed to have a knack for it even before then. My mother's family come from the desert. My father used to say I inherited my gift from them.'

The old man handed the carving back to Jabir and turned to the guard. 'Have the boy sent to my workshop.'

He walked out of the cell without another word to Jabir.

The prison guard jangled the keys at his belt. 'Hurry up, boy. It seems as if luck is on your side. You're free to go.'

CHAPTER FOUR

The Incredible
Clockmaker

Free! Just thinking of that word made Jabir gasp with relief. His prayers had been answered after all. His father had been right. The things you wanted didn't always happen in an instant but they eventually came true.

The prison guard showed Jabir to an outdoor trough, where he washed himself vigorously. The man in the exotic blue tunic had left a slave behind, a tall man with close-cropped hair and the bright blue eyes of the desert people. He introduced himself as Safir.

'Master wants to see you right away,' he said, and led Jabir down the street.

'What is your master's name?' asked Jabir, trying to keep up with the slave. It wasn't easy. Safir had long legs and walked with the speed of a gazelle.

'Master will tell you himself, if he chooses to,' replied Safir.

Jabir couldn't get another word out of him. They reached the end of the street and turned into the wide avenue where Jabir had been arrested. They crossed this and entered an even richer district where the houses were almost as big as palaces, with marble steps leading up to the front doors.

They came to the round city walls and exited through a gate different from the one Jabir had used to enter the city. 'This is known as the "Basra Gate",' said Sabir, 'because it faces the city of Basra across the desert.'

The desert didn't quite come up to the gate. Stepping through it, Jabir found himself in a sprawling suburb. The houses here were smaller than in the city, and more densely packed together. Most of the front doors were open, allowing the delicious smell of cooking to waft out. There was the clang of tools as men went about their work. Some of the houses were workshops. Jabir caught glimpses of men bent over their workbenches, hammering or sawing. There were shops selling everything from sweetmeats to leather bags and tools.

Safir led the way across several canals, each one filled with clean, flowing water. After the rank smell of prison, the outside air was sharp with the scent of citrus and Jabir guessed there were orchards beyond the gaggle of houses.

They reached a narrow street where Safir stopped to buy lakoum, a chewy sweet scented with rose water and dusted with icing sugar. Jabir had heard of it in tales but never tasted it. He watched as the sweet-seller wrapped it carefully in a piece of linen and handed it to Safir. Then they were off again, until they came to a large house with shuttered windows. Here

Safir produced a key and opened the door. 'Yasmina…?' he called.

A girl of about Jabir's age appeared out of the gloom. 'Safir? Have you brought the lakoum?'

'Yes, mistress.' Safir held out the linen-wrapped package.

'Thank you,' said Yasmina. 'Father will be pleased. He says he cannot work unless he has a constant supply of lakoum. I keep telling him so much sugar can't be good for his health. He is putting on weight, although you can't see it under his loose-flowing tunics. But you know how creative men are. They just ignore any advice they don't like.' She looked at Jabir. 'Is this him?'

'This is Jabir,' confirmed Safir.

Yasmina drew a veil across her face and smiled through the flimsy cloth. 'Welcome to our workshop, Jabir. Come along, Father is looking forward to seeing you. Safir, please make some mint tea and cut the lakoum into pieces. Father will be waiting for it.'

She turned and opened another door. It led into a surprisingly large workshop, its walls covered in charts and diagrams. There was a long workbench in the middle, draped in thick green cloth. Tools were lined up across it in precise, neat rows. A lamp burned at either end.

The man who had come to see Jabir in prison came forward. He still wore his beautiful tunic but he'd put on a leather apron to protect it, and he'd removed his turban. His hair was as white as his loose trousers. 'Welcome to my workshop, young man.'

'His name is Jabir,' said Yasmina.

'And I am Abu Mahfouz. I am a clockmaker—'

'The best clockmaker in Baghdad,' cut in Yasmina.

Her father frowned at her. 'Please show some humility, Yasmina. It is not fitting for a child to brag about her father.' He nodded at Jabir. 'Take a seat. Let me tell you why I freed you from prison. And you are not my slave, by the way. I did not pay for your freedom. When I heard from Mousa that you had been condemned to prison, I went to see the judge as soon as I could. I told him that if my hunch about you was correct, I might need your help for a very special project, one commissioned by the caliph Harun al-Rashid himself. It is very important for Baghdad and the world of Islam. Should you help me, you will be free to return home once our mission is complete. But fail me, and I am afraid the judge will insist you go back to prison.'

Safir came in with a tray of tea glasses and slices of the lakoum in a dish. He set them down on a small copper-topped table at the far end of the room.

'Sit, drink with us,' said Abu Mahfouz to Jabir, settling down on a leather cushion. 'I shall explain everything.' He picked a piece of lakoum. 'What do you know of Harun al-Rashid, our glorious caliph?'

Jabil's father had told him a lot about the famous caliph of Baghdad. His name meant Harun the Just, because he was fair and just with everyone brought before him. He was also a great lover of science, literature, music and art. In fact, he had built the most famous library in the world, the *Bayt al-Hikma* – the House of

Wisdom – where scholars worked day and night to translate ancient scripts from Greek and Latin.

'The caliph is very keen to make friends with Charlemagne, the Holy Roman Emperor and the most powerful man in Europe,' said Abu Mahfouz.

'Sadly, people in Europe tend to look down on us, the children of Islam. They have no idea of our great love for science and medicine. They know nothing about our passion for poetry, music and storytelling. They are unaware as yet that we have saved the knowledge of Ancient Greece and Rome from oblivion, and that our discoveries in science can help their own culture advance. The caliph is sending Charlemagne some gifts that will show his court, and the rest of Europe, how sophisticated our society is.'

Yasmina took over from her father. 'I have seen the list of presents and it's very impressive. The caliph is sending a real live elephant and bolts of fine cloth such as people in Europe have never seen. There will be costly perfumes, a jug and a tray made of pure gold, a set of chessmen, a tent the emperor can use when out hunting and a fine robe embroidered with the words "There Is But One God"—'

'But,' cut in Abu Mahfouz, unable to help himself, 'the most astounding gift is going to be a clock.' He unrolled a parchment to show Jabir a very complicated diagram of wheels and pistons surrounded by notes in flowing script. 'A water clock that the caliph has asked me to design especially for Charlemagne.'

Jabil frowned at the chart. 'What is a water clock?'

'It's a machine that tells the time of day, powered by water,' explained Yasmina.

Jabir, who counted the hours by the call to prayer and the movement of the sun across the sky, was astonished such a device could exist.

'It is going to be magnificent,' said Yasmina, unrolling another parchment. 'The best clock in the entire world, fit for an emperor. It will tell the time perfectly. Look, it is going to be shaped like a castle tower and have twelve brass balls hidden in a little box at the top. They will fall – one every hour – and hit a brass cymbal underneath to make a loud noise. At the same time, little golden horsemen will come out from the top of the tower and parade around the clock. There will be one for each hour. At one o'clock, one horseman will dance. At two, there will be two... and so on till the twelfth hour, when all twelve horsemen will trot out together and perform a dance. What do you think?'

Jabir looked up from the chart in wonder. 'I think it's magnificent, the most magical thing I have heard of. But... how can it work?'

'Father's clocks always work,' said Yasmina. 'That's why he's famous.'

'Humility, Yasmina, humility,' Abu Mahfouz reminded her, grabbing another piece of lakoum. He pointed it at Jabir. 'I want you to carve the horsemen in wood. When they are finished, we will take them to a gilder who will cover them in gold leaf.'

'Father will pay you a silver coin for every horse that you make,' added Yasmina. She consulted a beautifully drawn calendar on the workbench. 'We have twenty full days to finish the project. Then the caliph's caravan will set out to the city of Aachen in Europe with the gifts. What do you say?'

Jabil was so astonished by the offer, he could hardly speak. Twelve shiny silver coins! It was enough to pay off the landlord, see that his mother and sisters were taken care of and start a new life for himself, perhaps here in Baghdad itself. 'Yes, sir,' he spluttered, kissing Abu Mahfouz's hand. 'I will carve the horses for you. I am eternally grateful for this opportunity.'

Abu Mahfouz got to his feet. 'Let us shake hands on it, Jabir. May the great Allah – praise be on his holy name – guide our minds and hands.'

CHAPTER FIVE
The First Horseman

They finished the tea and Yasmina brought out more diagrams. These ones showed the twelve horsemen on their stallions and they were exquisite.

'I drew them myself,' she said. 'Father is very pleased with them.'

The horsemen were all the same size but differed in appearance so that none could be mistaken for another. Some wore turbans, others conical helmets with a spike on top. Their miniature weapons differed too. Some carried curved swords, others axes, javelins or bows and arrows.

'They are beautifully drawn,' commented Jabir. 'Your daughter is very talented, sir.'

'She is indeed,' agreed Abu Mahfouz, 'and I have no doubt that your own talents will match hers. But let us get to work at once. There is no time to lose.'

Yasmina nodded at Safir, who fetched a basket of chopped wood, placing it carefully on the workbench. They all gathered round it.

'Father thought you should carve the horsemen out of olive wood,' said Yasmina.

'It's the right choice,' said Jabir. 'Olive wood is fun to whittle and does not splinter readily, on account of the oil in it. It also keeps its shape for a long time and does not warp.'

Abu Mahfouz smiled. 'The boy knows what he's talking about.' He took a small knife out of a workbox. It was beautiful, with an ebony handle carved with elaborate script. 'Here, be careful with it. I've just had it sharpened.'

'I'd rather use my own whittling knife, *sayyid*,' said Jabir.

He took the sandal off his right foot and swung the heel round to reveal a hidden compartment. A small knife with a worn handle was lodged inside. 'My father gave it to me a long time ago,' he said, 'and I've become used to carving with it.'

Abu Mahfouz grinned. 'I use tools handed down to me from my ancestors too. Now, as for the clock…'

He called out to Safir, who opened a large chest and lifted out something hidden under a piece of purple cloth. He brought it to the workbench and put it down gently.

Abu Mahfouz whipped off the cloth. 'Behold, the clock that will astound the crowned heads of Europe.'

Jabir stared at the contraption. It was the most beautiful thing he'd ever seen. The square tower had two floors. The floor underneath had wide-open arches so that you could see inside. The floor was a round brass cymbal, polished till it shone. The upper floor had small doors all around it that opened on to a small balcony with a wooden railing.

'Is that where the horsemen will parade?' he asked.

Yasmina nodded. 'As father says, it will astound everyone in Europe who sees it.' She giggled. 'They'll never be able to work out how it functions, either. They'll think it's magic. Father is very clever with his inventions.'

'What gifts we have are given to us by the heavens,' sniffed Abu Mahfouz. 'We must use them so that we might glorify Allah – praise be on his holy name.' He turned to Jabir, who was still staring at the magnificent clock. 'Now, as regards living arrangements... This is not my house, it is just my workshop. Yasmina and I live in a villa within the city walls. But there are some humble living quarters upstairs. There's a kitchen, a bathroom and a small sitting room where you can relax. You can sleep under a canopy on the roof if you like. Safir will show you the way.'

'Does he live here too?' asked Jabir.

'No,' said Yasmina. 'Safir lives in our house in the city. Come, I'll show you upstairs myself.'

Even though Abu Mahfouz had said the living quarters were humble, to Jabir they felt like a palace. The sitting room had large windows that let in a cool breeze and could be shuttered during the heat of the day. The leather cushions were comfortable if a little worn, and there was a table with a water jug and food dishes. The bed under the canopy was a proper divan, with large pillows and cushions.

When Jabir came back down the stairs, Abu Mahfouz was putting on his turban. 'Are the rooms to your liking?' he asked.

'I've never dreamed of such luxury,' replied Jabir. 'Thank you very much, sir.'

Abu Mahfouz handed him a small purse. 'Here is some change for anything you might need. Safir will bring you your meals from the main house, and there is a well outside the back of the workshop where you can wash and draw water. Yasmina and I must go now. We have people coming to dinner. You can start carving right away. We shall see you bright and early tomorrow morning.'

Once the front door had closed, Jabir carried Yasmina's sketches upstairs. He lay in the shade of the canopy and studied them carefully. It was the first time he had handled parchment and he was almost in awe of it. To think you could put down your ideas on it and they remained there forever!

Jabir promised himself that he would learn to read and write. Then he could enjoy more than just pictures. He thought about sending his mother and sisters a message, to tell them that he was all right and well on the way to earning good money. But he had no idea where to find a scribe and a messenger he could trust. He would ask Yasmina in the morning.

He went downstairs to fetch some wood and spotted a sharpening block on the work-bench. He sharpened his knife and returned to the terrace upstairs. It was late afternoon. The sun was still bright in the sky but not harsh. The perfect light to whittle by. Jabir set to work on the first horseman. Yasmina had drawn him as a tall fellow with a long flowing beard and huge oval eyes. He looked almost real in the picture and Jabir was determined his carving would be just as good.

He soon became engrossed in his work and the sun had almost set by the time he put down his knife. There was a noise in the hallway and Safir came in with a basket of small dishes.

'Do you want to eat out here on the terrace?' he asked. 'It's a cool evening. I can fetch a lamp.'

'Yes, please,' said Jabir, wiping the knife on his sleeve. The blade was slippery with sweat and covered in sawdust. He stood the half-finished horseman on the palm of his hand and looked at it proudly. The figure gleamed in the light of Safir's lamp. Even though neither the horse nor the rider had facial features yet, they already looked magnificent.

'Master Abu was right,' said Safir. 'You are indeed talented. Now eat your dinner before it gets cold. I will put out the lamps downstairs on my way out. See you tomorrow.'

Safir went away. Jabir washed his hands then lifted the dishes out of the basket. A feast fit for a king awaited him. There was a fragrant stew scattered with pomegranate seeds, flatbread broken into pieces, and chopped ripe figs scattered in honeyed yoghurt.

Jabir stretched out on the divan to eat. He gorged himself till he thought his belly was going to burst. Then he washed and found a prayer mat for the last prayers of the day. It was dark now but Jabir was too excited to go to sleep. He picked up his knife again and continued working by lamplight.

When Safir brought Jabir's breakfast at dawn, he found the boy fast asleep with the whittling knife and the wooden horseman still in his hands. He removed them gently and looked closely at the horseman. It was finished already.

Safir carried it downstairs, where Abu Mahfouz and Yasmina had just arrived. He put it down on the workbench without saying a word and opened one of the shutters to let in the light. The early morning sun blazed in through the window, giving the horseman a life-like expression. He looked fierce, a club held tightly in one hand, the other pulling on the horse's reins.

'I wouldn't be at all surprised if it started cantering along the workbench,' gasped Yasmina. 'What do you think, Father?'

'My hunch about the boy was right,' said Abu Mahfouz. 'It is exquisite! The work of a true artist.'

CHAPTER SIX
The Grand Vizier

Over the next two days, Jabir carved two more horsemen. Now there were three of them lined up on the workbench for Abu Mahfouz to admire. The morning after the day of prayer, there was a knock on the workshop door.

'Who could that be?' wondered Abu Mahfouz, looking up from the clock, where he was working on the mechanism. 'I'm not expecting anyone.'

Yasmina went to answer it.

A tall man in a flowing white robe and an emerald-green turban came in. He had a fierce scowl but his eyes looked kind. Abu Mahfouz leaped to his feet at once. 'Welcome, *sayyid*. What an honour to see you in my workshop. Yasmina, some tea and sweetmeats, please.' He nodded to a carved divan. 'Rest your feet, your honour. To what do I owe the pleasure of this visit?'

'That is Ja'far ibn Yahya al-Barmaki, the grand vizier,' Yasmina whispered to Jabir when he followed her to the small back room where they kept the food and water. 'He is the caliph's most trusted man and he even persuaded him to open a paper mill here in Baghdad. He is a great patron of the sciences and he admires my father's work very much. I reckon it was him who convinced the caliph that Father should make the water clock for Charlemagne.'

'I have been sent to check on the clock's progress,' the vizier was saying as Yasmina and Jabir returned to the workshop. 'The caliph is very anxious that it should be finished on time.' Yasmina set down the tea and the sweetmeats while Jabir picked up the fourth horseman and continued whittling.

'I promise you the clock will be ready,' Abu Mahfouz assured the vizier. 'And a magnificent timepiece it will be too.' He nodded at the three horsemen on the workbench. 'Have a look at these.'

The vizier carried one of the carvings to the open window. He peered at it through a magnifying glass hanging on a gold chain around his neck, turning it over and over in his hand. 'But this is astounding work,' he said at last. 'Work no one in Europe could match, I'm sure. The caliph will be most pleased when he hears of your progress, Abu.'

'And here is the talented carver himself,' said Abu Mahfouz. 'He is working on the fourth horse as we speak.'

Jabir felt nervous as the vizier came closer and watched over his shoulder. He'd never been so close to a powerful person before. His whittling knife nearly slipped out of his hands but he steadied his nerves. The vizier didn't say a word until Jabir put down the half-finished horse to wipe the sweat from his forehead. Then he picked it up and ran his fingers slowly over the horse's mane.

'What is your name, boy?' he said at last.

'Jabir ibn Abdel, sir.'

'You have a glittering future ahead of you,' said the vizier. 'Perhaps you can carve me a chess set when you have finished working on the clock. How long did it take you to make the first three horsemen?'

'A night and two days,' replied Jabir.

'You must be working very hard,' said the vizier. He pulled out a purse from under his sash. 'Hard workers deserve a treat every now and then, Jabir. I know your good master is paying you to carve the horses but here is something extra as a token of my delight. Spend it on something luxurious for yourself.'

He thrust a coin into Jabir's hand.

'Thank you, *sayyid*,' whispered Jabir. He stared at the palm of his hand in disbelief. The vizier had given him a gold dinar.

CHAPTER SEVEN

The Landlord's Revenge

It was boiling hot on the road from Baghdad to the village but Jabir hardly noticed. He couldn't wait to give his mother the gold coin. She'd have enough to pay the rent for at least a year. The landlord's plans to evict them would come to nothing and Jabir's sisters would get new clothes. Especially Ayat. She would need some nice things to wear if she were ever going to make a good match.

The journey to the village and back would take up a full day and night but Jabir was confident he could make up for lost time. He planned to work on the horsemen every hour there was until they were all finished. It was a small price to pay for the joy of seeing his mother and sisters happy and safe from the landlord's dastardly plans.

Coming to the village, Jabir made his way to the fishermen's quarters. It was late in the day and people were getting up from their afternoon nap. Women were stoking the fires to prepare the evening meal.

Jabir found the door to their little house closed. *Strange*, he thought. His mother only ever closed the door on wintry nights when she thought the wind might blow evil spirits into the house. Usually it was left ajar to let in the breeze. Jabir tried the handle but the door was firmly locked. He banged on it with his fist. '*Umi*. Ayat. Nadya. Zubayda.'

There was no answer. He rattled the door handle, frustrated. 'Anyone in?'

He heard the hens clucking in the yard and went round to the back. The kitchen door was locked too. The washing line had been taken down from the fig tree.

'They're gone,' hissed a voice behind him. 'Your mother and sisters. They went away.'

Jabir turned to see their old neighbour looking out of a window. 'Gone where?'

'The landlord threw them out. He came round yesterday with his henchmen. They broke up the furniture and put new locks on the door.'

Rage made Jabir's blood rush to his head. 'That's not fair! We had until the full moon to pay him what we owed.'

'Such a cruel world we live in,' said the neighbour. 'Your mother left word with me. She and your sisters are staying in the cave on the other side of the river.'

The news made Jabir's eyes grow wide with horror. The cave on the other side of the river was a notorious place where the homeless ended up when they had nowhere else left to go. It was a filthy, wretched spot, full of disease.

Jabir thanked the neighbour for her help and hurried away, a plan forming in his mind. He would find the landlord and have it out with him. He'd pay the arrears and the rent, no matter how much the landlord asked for. Surely a greedy snake like him would not be able to turn down such a generous offer. Then Jabir would hire a boat to cross the river and rescue his mother and sisters. If he hurried, they would be safely back home tonight.

The landlord lived in the richer part of the village, in a big house surrounded by an orchard. It had a large wrought-iron gate that was usually locked. Jabir could hear the burbling of a fountain as he approached.

He pulled the bell chain and a startled flock of pigeons took off from the trees. An old man in a dirty blue robe came out of the main house.

'Yes?'

'I am here to see Yusuf Said.'

'Are you a tenant of his?'

'Yes.'

The man held out a hand. 'He is very busy at the moment. If you owe rent, leave the money with me and come back to speak with him tomorrow.'

'I need to speak to him now,' insisted Jabir. 'It's urgent. Surely he can spare a moment. My late father was a tenant of his for twelve years.'

'I told you, he is very busy,' said the man in the dirty robe. 'You can see him tomorrow.'

Jabir grunted with frustration. He had to get back to Baghdad before sunrise. And he couldn't bear the idea of his mother and sisters spending another night in that cave. He started clambering up the gate. The old man stepped away in alarm and shouted out for help. The door to the main house opened and someone else came out. An enormous man with muscled arms and a very small head.

'Farid! Is something the matter?'

'There's an intruder, Ibn Tufail,' shouted the man in the blue robe. 'I told him to go away but he won't.'

Jabir reached the top of the gate and leaped down inside the courtyard, landing in a clump of white lilies. Ibn Tufail yelled at the top of his voice, 'You there. Get out!'

Jabir ran straight at him like a mad bull. His head collided with his rock-hard belly, knocking him to the ground. Ibn Tufail tried to grab his leg but Jabir was too quick. He stepped over him and ran through the open door.

He heard someone burping loudly at the far end of a corridor and ran towards the noise. Yusuf Said was reclining on a carpet, eating dates. He lowered the dish. 'What on earth is going on?'

'It's me, sir. Jabir ibn Abdel. I need to speak with you. It's urgent. You threw my mother and sisters out of the house yesterday. Perhaps you forgot that you gave us until the full moon to pay our debts.' He held out the gold coin that the vizier had given him. 'Here. Take this. There's enough there to cover the rent for a long time. It'll match whatever you planned to charge the new tenants.'

The landlord stared at the coin but made no move to take it. 'I am knocking that house down to build a shop. The builders start work tomorrow.'

'But that's not fair,' argued Jabir. 'The house might belong to you but it is our home. My sisters and I were born in it. My father passed away there. All our memories, happy or sad, are tied up with that little house.'

'I could rent you another one,' said Yusuf Said, 'but you are such a troublemaker, I dare not let you into one of my properties again. And I suspect you stole that gold coin. You are a thief as well as a nuisance.'

Suddenly, something inside Jabir snapped. A troublemaker! A thief! It was the landlord who was all those things – not him. He leaped at Yusuf Said, kicking the dish out of his hands.

'*You* are the thief, sir. Everyone knows it. You stole my boat and my fishing net!'

By now the muscled henchman, Ibn Tufail, had come to the doorway.

'He tried to murder me,' snarled Yusuf Said. 'Get him out.'

Ibn Tufail's massive arms locked themselves around Jabir's chest and dragged him down the corridor to the front door. The man's grip was so powerful, Jabir thought his bones would crack. He winced at the pain but somehow he managed to twist his head round and face the henchman.

'Aaarghhh!' roared Ibn Tufail. He let go as Jabir spat right in his eye. By the time he'd wiped away the spit, cursing at the top of his voice, Jabir was halfway up the gate, with Farid trying in vain to grab him by the ankles.

Yusuf Said strode out to the porch, his eyes narrowed with rage. He watched as Jabir jumped down to the street. 'No one threatens me and lives,' he fumed at Ibn Tufail. 'Let the boy reach Baghdad. Then find him and kill him.'

CHAPTER EIGHT

The Rest of the Horsemen

Jabir got back to Baghdad just before sunrise, washed, said his prayers and was down in the workshop to greet Safir when he arrived with his breakfast.

After escaping from Yusuf Said's house, he had crossed the river to the cave where his mother and sisters had found shelter. Breaking the gold coin, he used some of the money to secure them a small house on the edge of the village. They could only live in it for a few weeks, while the usual tenants were away, but at least they were safe for the time being and Jabir could concentrate on finishing the rest of the horsemen.

He worked round the clock to meet the deadline, stopping only for meals, prayer times and a few hours of precious sleep under the canopy. Safir brought him a constant supply of treats to keep him going: fat dates stuffed with a paste of crushed nuts, fried dough dusted with sugar (the people of Baghdad seemed to put sugar on everything) and water biscuits spread with a smelly but delicious red cheese called kamakh ahmar.

Abu Mahfouz himself often came to watch Jabir work, keeping himself cool with a large hand-held fan while Safir served sweet mint tea in tiny sparkling glasses.

Sometimes Yasmina joined them, checking the wooden horsemen against her sketches to make sure the details were right. They always were, but Jabir added his own little details. He gave both the horses and the horsemen different facial expressions and he always made sure that they matched. If a horsemen looked happy, so did his horse. If a horse seemed bold or skittish, so did his master.

At last came the morning when Jabir placed the twelfth horseman on the workbench. He was the grandest one of all, with high cheekbones, a fierce moustache and a curved sword held high over his head. His horse had a spectacular tail that seemed to swish even as you looked at it.

'He will look magnificent covered in gold leaf,' said Abu Mahfouz, his voice husky with awe at Jabir's craftsmanship.

'It's taken just thirteen days for Jabir to complete the horsemen,' said Yasmina, checking the calendar. That leaves us seven days till the deadline, plenty of time for the gilding. We've done it, everyone!'

They had a celebratory cup of mint tea and a slice of lakoum, then Abu Mahfouz sent Safir to fetch the gilder.

'And not just any gilder,' Abu Mahfouz explained as they waited for the man to arrive.

'Ali Akbar is not only a personal friend of mine but also the most respected and highly paid gilder in the known world.'

* * *

Ali, a thin man with a slight hunch and puffy eyes, studied the horsemen for a long while, his lips pursed in concentration. 'This is very good work,' he said at last. 'It will be a pleasure to gild them. Who's the carver?'

Both Yasmina and her father pointed at Jabir. 'He's new to Baghdad,' said Abu Mahfouz, 'but I think you'll agree that his name will soon be famous all over the city.'

Jabir's chest swelled with pride. First Abu Mahfouz and Yasmina, then the grand vizier and now the most respected gilder in Baghdad had heaped praise on his work. For the first time in his life, he felt excited and optimistic about the future. He was doing something he had a passion for, something he was good at. And, most importantly, his family were safe. He was being a good provider like his father.

Ali laid out the tools of his trade on the counter: a piece of shark skin, browned with age; a pot of solidified rabbit-skin glue that he set on a small stove to melt; a jar of fragrant beeswax, a small knife with a sharp blade, and a pair of clean silk gloves. Then came several stiff horse-hair brushes and, last of all, sheets of pure gold nestled between the pages of an enormous ledger.

'Which horseman do you want me to gild first?' he asked Abu Mahfouz.

The clockmaker nodded at Jabir. 'They're your work. You choose.'

Jabir handed Ali the first one he'd carved, the fierce-looking fellow wielding a club. The gilder used the shark skin to smooth over the horseman, taking care not to erase the fine details of Jabir's carving. Then he put on the gloves and opened the ledger to select a sheet of gold leaf. He laid this carefully on the workbench and cut it into small neat squares with the knife.

Jabir and Yasmina stepped closer to watch.

'Make sure you don't sneeze or you'll blow the gold sheets away,' warned Ali. 'They're incredibly light and fragile.'

He covered the horseman's face with a thin layer of glue from the pot, then lifted one of the gold squares on the end of a brush and laid it in place. Gently he blew on it, forcing the thin layer of gold to mould itself around the horseman's intricate features. Jabir thought it was like watching magic, seeing wood turn to gold.

Ali stopped only for a moment to take a sip of tea before gilding the rest of the horseman. The sun was low in the sky by the time he placed the finished carving on the workbench.

'I will wait until the glue is dry, and then I shall give the gold a thin coating of beeswax to protect it and make it shine even more,' said Ali. 'It's getting too late to start gilding another. I'll be back tomorrow. You can help me, Jabir, and you too, Yasmina. You both have very steady hands. He started putting away his tools. I'm sure you'll be as good at gilding as you are at carving and drawing.'

Over the next three days Ali, helped by Yasmina and Jabir, worked tirelessly on gilding the horsemen. It was Thursday evening, before the end of day prayers, when they put down their pots of beeswax and stepped away from the counter. They had been concentrating so hard on their work that they hadn't noticed the light fading.

'We've done it,' said Jabir, wiping the sweat off his face.

'With four days to spare,' said Abu Mahfouz. 'This calls for a celebration.' He'd been painting a garland of flowers around the base of the clock but he was not yet finished. 'Safir, you take the clock to my house. Put it in my room. Take my paints and brushes too. I'll finish the flowers before I retire tonight.'

He turned to the others. 'I'm treating you all to a banquet at the best cookhouse in Baghdad, an establishment run by one of the most famous recipe collectors in the world, Sayyar Ali. I have been there many times and I can guarantee you the food is superb. But first let's perform our prayers. We need to thank Allah for his blessings and generosity.'

They all washed, then Jabir and Abu spread their mats on the workshop floor while Yasmina went to pray up on the terrace. Their prayers done, Abu Mahfouz locked the precious horsemen in a chest. Jabir and Yasmina carefully extinguished the lamps and Abu Mahfouz let them out.

The sun had set but children were still playing in the street. A donkey cart was rumbling down the road away from the house.

'The rubbish collectors are awfully late today,' said Yasmina.

The cart driver was an enormous man with very long hair that hid most of his face. He stooped to whisper in the donkey's ear as Jabir walked past. Another man was shuffling behind him, emptying baskets of rubbish on to the cart.

The famous cookhouse stood at the end of a very narrow street outside the city walls. Sayyar, the proprietor, was a short man wearing a ridiculously huge turban encrusted with pearls. He came out to greet them himself.

'Welcome to my humble establishment, esteemed clients,' he wheezed, bowing so low his beard nearly touched the floor. 'I have a place for you on my most comfortable divans.'

He pulled aside a red curtain to reveal a small room with two divans covered in plump cushions. A round table with a brass top stood between them.

'What shall I get you to drink?' asked Sayyar when he'd shown everyone where to sit. 'Camel's milk with honey? Sherbet?'

They all chose the sherbet, which was a delicious mix of crushed fruit and herbs.

'But what food have you got for us, Sayyar?' asked Abu Mahfouz.

'Tonight, my cooks have prepared such dishes as you could only read about in *One Thousand and One Nights* till I worked out the recipes,' boasted Sayyar. 'We have chicken stewed with plums and almonds. Flatbreads kneaded with crushed olives and rosemary. Jewelled couscous and a tagine of spiced vegetables.'

'We shall taste them all,' laughed Abu Mahfouz.

Sayyad clapped to summon assistants and bowed again before leaving the room.

'The man might look ridiculous in that turban,' declared Abu Mahfouz, as the sherbets were served. 'But he has the biggest collection of recipe books in the world and his chief cook once worked for the King of Persia. I believe he has a certificate to prove it.'

The food was indeed delicious and Jabir dipped chunks of flatbread in the various dishes many times. When the round table was cleared away and Sayyar had brought in a tray of sweetened mint tea, Abu Mahfouz sat up on the divan.

'You have done me proud, Jabir,' he said. 'I was so lucky to spot you in the music merchant's house the night you were accused of stealing food. I couldn't have hoped for finer horsemen to go on my clock. I'm sure the caliph will be as pleased with them as me, and so will the Emperor Charlemagne in the city of Aachen.'

'Thank you, sir,' said Jabir, his face going red with embarrassment. 'I was indeed lucky you spotted me. I would still be rotting in prison if you hadn't rescued me. And, of course, Yasmina's beautiful drawings were an inspiration and Ali's gold leaf makes my work look much better than it really is.'

'You have a rare gift,' said Abu Mahfouz. 'Use it wisely and you'll soon be a rich man. Once the caliph approves of your work, you will have people flocking to your door for commissions.' He reached under his sash and thrust a purse into Jabir's hands.

'Here's your payment. Twelve silver dirhams, one for every horseman as promised. Count them to be sure I've made no mistakes.'

'Thank you, sir. I am very grateful.' Jabir put the purse in his pocket without examining its contents. It was something he'd often seen his father doing when getting paid for his catch, a sign of trust.

Ali got to his feet. 'Well, friends, I'm calling it a night. Abu, thanks for such a wonderful feast.'

Sayyar held the door open for them as they filed out, burping loudly to show they had enjoyed the food. He did not ask Abu Mahfouz for payment. As a regular customer, he had credit with the cookhouse. Jabir promised himself that he would be a regular customer of Sayyar's one day too. He would bring his family for a meal and sherbets. His sisters would dine like Persian princesses.

Jabir said goodbye as the others headed one way towards the wide avenues where the rich people lived and he turned back to the city gates towards the workshop. The silver dirhams clinked in his purse.

On the terrace, he lay on the divan and enjoyed the cool night breeze. The sound of a guitara carried from the house across the alley. One of the neighbours was singing his children a lullaby.

The night draws a veil on the day
The sun hides her face
The moon awakens
Come, my little ones
Let us fly like swallows
to the desert.
There the sand remembers

The ancient names of your grandfathers.
The palm trees will whisper
They will teach you secrets
Only your ancestors knew.

Jabir thought of his mother singing a lullaby to Nadya and Zubayda in their new home. He looked up at the stars winking in the sky and thanked Allah once again for his extreme generosity. It had been an extraordinary and a fulfilling day.

CHAPTER NINE

Fire!

Jabir woke up in the middle of the night, a faint sense of alarm ringing in his head. There was a strange smell and something tickled his nose and the back of his throat. Smoke! Suddenly he became aware of an intense heat coming out of the workshop. Jabir leaped out of bed, panic rising in his chest. Black smoke billowed out of the terrace doorway. The workshop was on fire.

Jabir's first thought was of the golden horsemen. He had to save them. He tore the sheet off the bed, thrust it into the bowl of water he used for his ablutions and draped it over his head. The small sitting room was not yet on fire but it was thick with smoke. Foolishly, Jabir forced himself to enter, peering through the wet sheet held against his face. The thick smoke and intense heat pushed him back. Even as he watched, the door at the top of the stairs fell in, exposing an inferno of roaring flames. There was no chance of saving the horsemen after all. They would be burnt to cinders already, the gold leaf melted.

Jabir retreated to the relative safety of the roof terrace.

'Son, are you there? Show yourself if you are.'

Someone was calling from below. Jabir leaned over the parapet.

'Yes, I'm here.'

A sea of worried faces was staring up at him. The man who had called out was the neighbour with the guitara. 'Are you alone?'

'Yes,' said Jabir. 'I'm the only one here.'

'You need to get down before it's too late,' called the neighbour. 'The building might collapse at any time. Can you leap across the alleyway to my roof?'

Jabir looked at the house opposite. It had always seemed so close but now it looked terribly far away. Still, he had no choice. Throwing off the wet sheet, he clambered on to the parapet, balanced there for a second, then threw himself across the street. He caught his foot on the parapet opposite but tumbled safely on to the roof tiles. A door opened and the kind neighbour and his family came rushing out. 'Are you all right?'

Jabir clambered to his feet. 'I'm fine, thanks.'

'Come on,' urged the neighbour. 'It's not safe here either. The fire might spread over to our house too.'

Jabir hurried after the family down narrow stairs and out on to the street. It seemed the whole of Baghdad was there. People were rushing around with basins of water, but Jabir knew it was too late to save the workshop.

'How did the fire start?' Jabir asked the neighbour. 'I'm sure I put out all the lamps before I went to bed.'

'They're saying it's arson,' said the neighbour's wife, rocking a child in her arms. 'Two strangers were seen lurking outside the workshop, pretending to be rubbish collectors. And someone heard a loud crash just after midnight. When they looked outside, one of the workshop's windows was smashed and the strangers were nowhere to be seen. They must have chucked a pot of burning oil in it through the window.'

The image of the dust cart and the two men collecting rubbish flashed through Jabir's mind. And suddenly he realised he'd seen both men before. The enormous one was Ibn Tufail, the weedy one Farid. The landlord's henchmen! They'd been keeping watch on the workshop. And they'd set the place on fire, hoping to kill him. It was their master's revenge on an insolent boy who had mocked him.

Jabir sank to his knees in guilt and shame. It was his fault that the twelve golden horsemen had been destroyed. He had led Yusuf Said's men to the workshop. Because of him Yasmina and her father were ruined and the caliph's clock would never be finished.

CHAPTER TEN
A Brilliant Idea

Jabir sat on the edge of a divan in Abu Mahfouz's house. The clockmaker, his daughter and Safir had all come running when they heard the workshop was on fire. They were relieved to find Jabir safe and sound.

'It's my fault the place was burned down,' cried Jabir. 'You've lost your workshop, your books and your tools.'

'No it's not.' Yasmina put an arm round his shoulders. 'How were you to know those evil men would set the place on fire?'

'But I've told you the story,' said Jabir. 'I angered their master and this is his revenge.'

'Those men are criminals,' said Yasmina. 'They will be hauled in front of a judge when my father catches up with them.'

'I shall not stop until those men get punished,' stormed Abu Mahfouz. 'And their master too, if he's behind this. Do not worry about my workshop, Jabir. We'll build a new one, and everything in it can be replaced. It's the golden horsemen we need to think about. Luckily, the water clock was at my house so it's safe, but we need twelve new horsemen.'

'We have four days left before we are due to present the clock to the caliph,' said Yasmina.

'It took me ten days to carve all the horsemen,' said Jabir. 'And another three days for Ali to gild them. We're doomed.'

Yasmina smiled. 'My late mother, may her spirit rest in eternal peace, used to say this: when you're faced with a terrible dilemma, first you need to pray, to make *dua*.'

'I know that,' said Jabir, 'but did she tell you what to do next?'

'You find a quiet spot,' replied Yasmina. 'Away from any noise and bustle, where you can think – hard, until you find a solution to your problem.'

Abu Mahfouz smiled sadly. 'I remember your mother repeating that often, especially when she and I were young and poor. They were good words of advice, my daughter, and you would do well to heed them. I will go and see the grand vizier. He will have heard of the fire by now and I must reassure him that everything will be fine. You two put your heads together. We need to find a solution to our dilemma. By tonight!'

*　　*　　*

It was the time of the day prayer, so Jabir hurried to the mosque. He prayed fervently, never doubting for a moment that Allah would help him sort out the problem. Returning home, he found

Yasmina putting away her prayer mat. He felt calm, as he always did after going to the mosque.

Yasmina made mint tea and they carried their glasses outside. Abu Mahfouz's house had a large courtyard with a tinkling fountain. There were stone benches on either side of it, one sheltered by an ancient jasmine, the other by a trailing rose bush.

Yasmina sat under the jasmine while Jabir took the seat under the rose. The air was heavy with scent and it made him sort of sleepy. He relaxed and lay back, trying to think. After a while the sound of splashing water became faint and distant. Jabir closed his eyes. He was so relaxed, he thought he might fall asleep.

But he didn't.

Instead his mind became more alert and he focused on the problem at hand. He had to carve twelve wooden horsemen, and he had to do it in just over two days, giving Ali one day to gild them all. It seemed impossible. Neither he nor Ali could work fast enough, even if they stayed up all night.

A little voice whispered at the back of his mind: *If you can't carve the horsemen on time on your own, then you must seek help.*

Ha, thought Jabir. But where can I get help?

The little voice at the back of his mind whispered again:

The night draws a veil on the day
The sun hides her face
The moon awakens
Come, my little ones
Let us fly like swallows
to the desert.
There the sand remembers
The ancient names of your grandfathers.
The palm trees will whisper
They will teach you secrets
Only your ancestors knew.

It was the lullaby that Jabir had heard the neighbour sing. The one about the ancestors in the desert. And suddenly the words gave him a solution.

His mother's people lived in the desert. And what had his father said many a time about his whittling? 'You inherit your gift from your mother's side of the family. They are all talented carvers.' Well, Jabir would find his desert family. They would help him carve the horsemen. If they all worked together, they could finish them on time. He'd pay them with his silver dirhams. As for the gilding, he would leave that in Allah's generous hands.

Jabir sat up so quickly it made him dizzy. 'Yasmina,' he said. 'I have an idea...'

CHAPTER ELEVEN
To the Desert

Now that Jabir had a clear plan to follow, he found himself charged with energy. Yasmina was just as enthusiastic but full of questions. 'How will we know where to find your family? How will we recognise your relatives if you've never even met them? Will they recognise you? Are you sure they will agree to help?'

'The family ties and obligations in desert families run deep,' Jabir assured her. 'It's how they survive in a hostile environment. They'll help. As for the other questions, we'll ask my mother. I know they're difficult to contact but she'll find a way.'

Yasmina was a capable horse rider and had a white Arab mare. Jabir helped her saddle it and they set off to his village, riding so fast they covered the long journey in only two hours. His mother and the twins were overawed with Yasmina. The girls had never seen such a beautiful girl before, especially not one who rode a horse. Her veil, spangled with coloured glass beads, made her look like a princess out of a fairy tale.

Yasmina put them at ease by giving them cakes and telling jokes. Ayat brought out welcoming cups of tea.

'What brings you back home so soon, *abnay*?' asked Jabir's mother.

Jabir told her about the golden horsemen and the fire. His mother's eyes grew wide with horror. '*Abnay*, I pray every day that you might come to no harm. I am glad my prayers have been answered. But take care, Yusuf Said is heartless. He has hated this family for as long as I can remember.'

'But why?' Jabir wanted to know. 'It is not normal for someone to hate so much.'

'Let us talk of more positive things,' said his mother. 'Tell me how you mean to solve your problem.'

Jabir explained his plan to find his relatives and ask them to help carve new horsemen.

'You are in luck, *abnay*,' said his mother. 'This is the time of year when our people, the Badawi, come together to organise a beauty contest for their camels.'

Yasmina raised an eyebrow and the twins immediately copied her. 'A beauty contest for camels?'

Jabir's mother smiled. 'Some camels are more beautiful than others and these fetch a higher price at the market. The men especially are very keen to own beautiful camels and the competition at the festival gets fierce. Foolish men have been known to challenge each other to duels when their own camels are not judged the best-looking. The festival is taking place as we speak. If you hurry you might still find the

Badawi celebrating. Our own family is sure to be there. They never miss a camel beauty contest.'

'But how will we find them?' asked Jabir.

'The festival takes place near a wadi called the Valley of Bones. It is also a place where spice caravans meet to exchange goods, money and gossip.'

'I have heard tell of such a place,' said Yasmina. 'My father has spoken of it before. We'll find someone to take us there.' She stood up and replaced the veil on her face. '*Shukran* to all the family. We must get going.'

Jabir's mother opened a chest and drew out a black shawl with red patterns all over it. 'I wore this at my wedding. My mother will recognise it at once. It belonged to her before me.'

She wrapped the shawl in a piece of cotton and placed it Yasmina's hands.

'I will take good care of it, and bring it back,' said Yasmina. 'I promise.'

Jabir's mother nodded and smiled. 'My blessings go with you, children, and may Allah guide your steps.'

*　*　*

Back in Baghdad, Abu Mahfouz set about finding a desert guide to take Jabir and Yasmina into the desert.

'I should come with you,' he fussed.

'The last time you went to the desert you came back almost dead,' chided Yasmina. 'The desert sun is too hot for you.'

'Ah yes,' said Abu Mahfouz sadly. 'I went to take part in a falconry contest. I used to keep falcons in those days and agile hunters they were too. They won me a prize but sadly I was too ill to attend the prize-giving ceremony.'

'Mother used to say you get sunstroke very easily,' admonished Yasmina. 'I'm sorry, but you can't come with us, Father. You'll only hold us up. Why don't you go and see the vizier? Ask him if the caliph can wait a couple more days for the clock. That will give Ali enough time to gild the new horsemen.'

'Very well,' sighed Abu Mahfouz. 'But I shall hire the best guide in Baghdad for you, and the most docile camels to take you to the Valley of Bones. Come with me, Jabir.'

Safir led them to a part of the city where the camel merchants lived. Abu Mahfouz knocked on a door. It was answered by a young servant who showed them into a spacious sitting room with striped divans.

'This is my old friend Baki's house,' said Abu Mahfouz.

Baki was a retired caravan owner. He had often brought Abu Mahfouz pearls from other countries for his clocks. He still bred camels and took his guests to the stables where he chose the two most tame ones for Jabir and Yasmina.

'Will you act as their guide too, my friend?' Abu Mahfouz asked Baki.

The retired merchant smiled. 'I would be honoured.'

It took the rest of the afternoon to prepare for the journey. Baki instructed the children to bring warm clothes for the night. It got freezing cold in the desert once the sun went down. And they needed leather flasks full of water, and food that would not spoil in the heat.

Abu Mahfouz rode with them to the edge of the desert. He called out a blessing as they set off across the sand. It was a clear night. The sky shimmered with bright stars, which Baki used as a compass.

'What will guide us when the sun rises and the stars disappear?' asked Jabir.

'Oh, I know the answer to that one,' said Yasmina. 'I read about it in a book. We follow the footsteps left by other travellers. Is that not true, Baki?'

'It is,' replied the guide, 'and you must be careful not to stray from the path. The desert people often dig pits in the sand to trap lions. Often you can't see them because they're camouflaged with reeds and saplings.'

Jabir looked around him alarm. If there was a lion trap nearby, he wanted to make sure he didn't fall into it. The desert was both magical and scary, he decided. The sand stretched out in every direction, glowing a luminous white in the starlight. It seemed silent, yet if you listened carefully you could hear all kinds of secret noises. Things scurrying through the sand, the wind moaning like a lost soul in the stunted bushes.

When the sun rose, flooding the desert with a rosy light, Jabir was surprised at how many marks in the sand the night creatures had left. There were paw prints made by four-footed animals and meandering curves left by snakes and lizards' tails.

They had a breakfast of dates and water, then moved swiftly on, eager to get to the Valley of Bones. They stopped only once at an oasis to eat a bigger meal of dried meat and flatbread, which Baki made fresh over a fire.

'Why is the wadi we're going to called the Valley of Bones?' Jabir asked as they ate in the shade of a palm tree.

Baki spoke through a mouthful of bread. 'It has a big watering hole where many caravans stop to rest and feed their camels. A long time ago, an enemy of the Badawi poisoned the water and many died. The ground was littered with the bones of people and camels. They say the people's spirits wander the desert still.'

'But is the water safe to drink now?' asked Yasmina.

Baki wiped his mouth with the edge of his scarf. 'It has been for a long time. There is nothing to fear. I have drunk from it often.'

They refilled their goatskins and got back on their camels. Late in the afternoon, they heard the sound of laughter beyond the dunes.

'We're nearly there,' said Baki. 'Behold, the Valley of Bones.'

CHAPTER TWELVE
Grandma Nabiha

'Visitors!' The shout carried across the sand. Someone on a camel was keeping watch at the top of the nearest dune.

Baki held up his hand in greeting. '*Marhaba!*'

The guard waved back. A moment later he was joined by other people on foot. They came running down the dune and swarmed around Jabir and Yasmina.

'*Marhaba!* Are you here for the camel beauty contest? If so, you are late. It ended yesterday.'

'We are looking for my family,' said Jabir, removing the scarf from around his face to speak. 'I am Jabir ibn Abdel. My father married Ameena of the Badawi.'

'If your mother is Ameena who married the fisherman from the Tigris, we are cousins,' said one of the boys. 'My mother is her sister. Come, cousin, I will show you where we are camped.'

They came to the top of the dune and Jabir saw a wadi stretched out below him, with dozens of tents pitched in neat rows. Beyond them, he could make out a watering hole surrounded by date palms. Smoke rose from fires here and there and the smell of cooking meat carried on the breeze. Children were chasing each other around the tents and men were feeding the camels.

'My name is Saleh,' said the boy. 'I will take you to Grandma Nabiha. She is the oldest woman in the family and our leader. Her tent is the biggest in the whole tribe. Come with me.'

While Baki led the camels to the watering hole, Jabir and Yasmina followed Saleh to a very large tent held up with thick poles. The entrance was covered with colourful rugs hung like curtains. A whole crowd of onlookers had gathered around it, smiling and nodding encouragingly at the strangers. Saleh parted the rugs. 'Grandma, we have a special visitor.'

'Is it a camel-seller?' replied a gruff voice. 'If so, tell him to go away. We have enough camels.'

'It is not a camel-seller,' replied Saleh. 'It is a relative from Baghdad, a Badawi.'

There was silence for a moment, then Grandma Nabiha called out, 'Bring him in. If he has brought someone with him, bring them in too. No one is ever turned away from Nabiha the Elder's tent.'

Saleh nodded at Jabir and Yasmina, inviting them inside. They removed their sandals as they entered, a sign of respect they knew all desert people appreciated. Their feet sank into a soft rug and they heard the murmur of voices.

A line of women sat under an enormous wicker fan, which moved slowly back and forth, creating a welcoming breeze. The one in the middle gestured to the ones on either side of her and they helped her to her feet.

She was a tiny woman, barely five feet tall and stooped with age. Her face was a mass of deep wrinkles but her teeth were a pure snowy-white and her blue eyes were clear and sharp. She lifted a hand and gently caressed Jabir's face. 'It is like my Ameena come back to me,' she whispered, her voice cracking with emotion. 'You must be Jabir, my grandson.'

Jabir held up the black and red scarf. 'My mother said you would recognise me by this.'

'But I do not need a wedding scarf to recognise you,' muttered Grandma Nabiha. 'You have your mother's eyes and lips. *My* eyes and lips.'

She drew Jabir into her arms and hugged him tight. The other women made an eerie howling sound which, Jabir knew, was to show their joy and respect.

'This is my friend Yasmina,' he said. 'Her father is a clockmaker from Baghdad.'

'Welcome, Yasmina,' replied Grandma Nabiha. 'These women are all Jabir's aunts and cousins.' She clapped her hands. 'Bring tea and dates. The poor children must be famished.'

She invited Jabir and Yasmina to sit on big, beautifully embroidered cushions. 'Tell me about your mother and sisters, Jabir. Are they well?'

'They are well, may Allah be praised,' said Jabir. 'But, Grandma, Yasmina and I have come to ask for your help. We are in deep trouble…'

A look of concern came into Grandma Nabiha's eyes. 'Tell me all.'

The other women gathered round as Jabir told them about his adventure, starting with the night Yusuf Said had threatened to have them thrown out of their home.

'That man always was a snake in the sand,' spat Grandma Nabiha. 'We had him thrown out of the tribe. But tell me more…'

'You know Yusuf Said?' gasped Jabir.

'He is a Badawi, like you,' replied Grandma Nabiha, 'a bad one. Tell me more about your misfortunes.'

When Jabir finished his story, Grandma Nabiha nodded at one of the women in the circle. 'Fetch me my walking stick.'

The woman brought the stick. It was curved like a crescent moon, worn with age and shiny with oil. Its handle was decorated with two falcons, their wings wrapped around each other.

'My husband carved me this for our wedding,' said Grandma Nabiha, holding it out for Yasmina and Jabir to admire. 'Have you ever seen a finer piece of carving? It is the envy of the desert. Your evil landlord shall not triumph. We shall carve the twelve golden horsemen for you, and we shall do it in only one night.'

CHAPTER THIRTEEN

The Night of the Carvers

Grandma Nabiha walked out of the tent, leaning on her beautiful walking stick. When she returned, she had a tall man with her. She introduced him as Utbah, the best whittler of the Badawi.

'I am a cousin of your mother's,' Utbah told Jabir. 'Grandma has told me about your dilemma. I shall try to help you. Have you any sketches of the horsemen?'

'Sadly, they were destroyed by the fire,' said Yasmina, 'but give me some time and I will sketch them again. They won't be as finely drawn as the originals but they'll be good enough to work with.'

She drew parchment and a stick of charcoal from her bag and started sketching. 'These are fine illustrations,' said Utbah as Yasmina finished one sketch after another. 'It will be an honour to carve the horsemen. News of your problem has spread around the camp and everyone wants to help, but I shall choose only the finest whittlers.' He placed a finger on the picture of the horseman with the curved sword. 'I shall carve this one myself.'

'And I shall work on this one,' said Jabir, pointing to the first horseman he'd carved, the one with the club.

Utbah handed one of the sketches to Saleh. 'You can whittle this one. I shall gather the rest of the carvers.'

News of the carving had indeed spread around the camp like wildfire and the air echoed with excited chatter. The women stoked up the fire outside Grandma Nabiha's tent and put a goat on the roasting spit. They sang as they chopped vegetables for salad and pounded spice for the pot. There would be a grand feast when the work was finished.

Umi, Umi
Where's my bridegroom?
Gone chasing fat gazelle and hare.
Binti, Binti
He's returning
We'll have food enough to spare.

The men brought twelve stools and placed them in two lines outside the tent. One of them had brought a basket of chopped olive wood too. He put it on the ground between the lines, along with a sharpening block and a pot of oil.

Soon Utbah had returned with the rest of the carvers, three men and six women. They all sharpened their whittling knives, wetting them in the oil before rubbing their blunt edges against the block.

'A golden dinar for the one to finish his horseman first,' cried Grandma Nabiha, settling at the entrance to her tent to watch. 'May Allah guide your knives.'

Silence fell on the camp as the whittlers set to work. Night fell, bringing a chill breeze with it. No one seemed to notice. The children kept adding logs to the fire and its bright glow shone on the carvers' sweaty faces. They stopped only for moments now and then, to change the position of the whittling knife in their hand or to consult the sketches on the ground before them.

Yasmina watched Jabir. He frowned as he worked, the wood chippings flying from his carving. 'Jabir, you want something to eat or drink?'

He was concentrating so hard, he didn't even hear her. The sky had turned a muted pink by the time one of the carvers stood up. It was a woman called Zahara. 'I've finished,' she cried. 'I've finished – look!' She held out her horseman and people rushed forward to see.

'It is beautiful, Zahara. Show it to Grandma. Show it to everyone.'

Zahara carried the horseman to the big tent. 'The best carving you've done yet, my child,' declared Grandma Nabiha, her teeth sparkling. 'You are the winner of the gold coin.'

One by one the rest of the carvers finished their own pieces. They placed them in a basket lined with a silk cushion that Grandma Nabiha had brought out. Jabir stared at them in awe. They were all expertly carved, perhaps even better than the ones he had made.

He offered up a silent prayer of thanks. With a bit of luck, he and Yasmina would return to Baghdad by the following morning. If only Abu Mahfouz and the vizier had convinced the caliph to wait a few more days for the clock, everything would be fine...

Jabir offered up a second prayer. Allah had helped him once. He would surely do so again.

Grandma Nabiha put the basket in his hands. 'Here you are, my child. The work is done. Once again the Badawis have come together to protect their own. Will you stay and feast with us before you go? We will dance in your honour.'

'We have a long journey ahead of us and much work to do still,' replied Jabir. 'We'd better start at once.'

Grandma Nabiha nodded. 'I understand. May you have safe passage across the desert. Give my love to your mother and your sisters. And come and see us again soon.'

Baki appeared with the camels and Yasmina and Jabir got into the saddles. The rest of the tribe ululated their goodbyes. The last Jabir saw of the camp was his extended family gathered around the fire to eat breakfast. Music drifted across the sand and there was the sound of fast, rhythmic clapping and music. His cousins had started to dance and they would go on dancing all day. Grandma Nabiha stood apart from the family, waving goodbye with her curved stick.

CHAPTER FOURTEEN
The Snake in the Sand

They rode all day, Baki urging the camels on with soft words and strange clicks he made with his tongue and lips. It was suprising how fast camels moved when they wanted to.

When the sun set, they ate on the hoof so as not to waste time. Jabir was sore from sitting in the saddle for so long. His arms felt as if they would fall off any moment. As dawn approached, Baki stopped them for a short rest. They were ready to set off again when the ground started to shake and a gigantic cloud of dust rose up ahead.

'What is that?' Jabir asked Baki.

'It must be a spice caravan,' cried Yasmina. 'It's coming from the direction of Baghdad.'

They watched the caravan materialise out of the sand as if by magic. There seemed to be hundreds of camels, the young ones trotting close to their mothers on spindly legs. The adult beasts were laden with enormous chests and wicker baskets dangling from their humps. The smaller camels carried rolled-up rugs or bales of wool. Their owners walked beside their camels although the elderly and the important took up precious space on the creatures' backs.

'They're on their way to trading ports in North Africa,' said Baki. 'From there the goods will sail on to Europe. Look at them. They're carrying everything Baghdad has to offer. Silk, glass lamps, rugs, paper, books, dyes for cloth, dates picked early to mature on the way, even ceramic tiles for the palaces of the rich.'

'And there are exotic things brought to Baghdad from countries even further to the east of our country. They were carried along the River Tigris,' added Yasmina, who had read about caravans in her father's geography books. 'Spices from India, myrrh and incense. Cardamom and saffron, to sweeten and colour the food of Europe's wealthy merchants and landowners. You can smell their rich fragrance above the stench of camel dung if you sniff long enough.'

When the caravan had passed and the sand had settled again, they refilled their goatskins and got back in the saddle. The sun was scorching, even that early in the morning, and they moved at a slow pace. Suddenly Baki put a hand to stop them.

'What's the matter?' whispered Yasmina, pulling on her reins.

'I've just heard a camel grunt.'

Jabir peered around him. 'I see no camels.'

'Look at that huge boulder over there,' said Baki. 'There's someone hiding behind it. You can see his shadow on the ground.'

'And there's someone else hiding behind that rock on the other side of the path,' added Yasmina. 'I can see their shadow too.'

'Are they hiding from us?' asked Jabir.

'No,' replied Baki. 'I think they're lying in wait for us.'

Even before he'd finished speaking, one of the shadows moved and a man on a camel strode out from behind the rock. He had a scarf wrapped around his face but there was no mistaking those hate-filled eyes. It was Yusuf Said, the landlord.

He was joined by the man behind the second rock. Ibn Tufail! The two men advanced menacingly on Jabir and Yasmina.

'You thought you'd outwit me,' Yusuf Said sneered at Jabir. 'But I have spies everywhere, even in the desert, and they sent me a messenger dove. So I found out all about the new horsemen that your precious family helped carve, and I knew that if I followed that caravan, it would lead me to you. I want to make sure the caliph will never see those horsemen. And you shall never become the famous carver you wish to be.'

'Why do you hate me so much?' cried Jabir. 'I can't be the only tenant who fell behind with the rent? Why pick on me?'

Yusuf Said spat on the ground. 'Did your precious mother not tell you? She was promised to me, but she married another. She shamed me. I swore on her wedding day that I would not let her and her family know any peace as long as I live.'

Jabir's mind reeled at the news. His mother promised to Yusuf the landlord? No, it couldn't be true.

'I see the news has alarmed you,' cackled Yusuf Said. 'I would say, ask your mother to tell you the whole story when you get home – she'll tell you about the gifts I sent her, all of which she refused. But, of course, you're not going to get back home and ask questions. You're going to die out here in the desert. Your mother will spend the rest of her miserable life in mourning for you and your father. How do you think he died, by the way? Did he fall over the side of his rickety little boat, or was he pushed?'

He whipped out a curved sword and Ibn Tufail did the same. 'Now hand over those twelve horsemen. I want the luxury of destroying them with my own hands.'

'He doesn't have them,' replied Baki. 'They're safely in my saddlebag. And no one is going to take them from me.'

'Aren't they?' snickered Yusuf Said. He urged his camel slowly forward. Out of the corner of his eye, Jabir spotted Ibn Tufail advance on Baki from behind. The two were going to trap the guide between them. He flicked the reins on his camel, intending to rush to Baki's side, but Yasmina placed a hand gently on his.

'Let Baki deal with this. I am sure he's faced worse enemies.'

As she spoke, Baki reached behind his back and very slowly drew out a dagger from between his shoulder blades.

Yusuf Said laughed. 'Nice place to hide a weapon. But is that all you have to defend yourself with? A little knife? My father used to open letters with a weapon like that.'

Baki tightened his grip on the dagger's hilt. There was a surprisingly loud click and two side daggers sprang out from behind the main one, forming a trident.

'Three daggers enough for you?' he spat. He leaped off his camel in one smooth movement and landed right by Yusuf Said. The landlord was rattled for a moment but then he too jumped to the ground. The sharp clang of steel rang out as the two men fought. Ibn Tufail, who was still in the saddle, inched his camel forward. Suddenly he grunted. An astonished look flashed in his eyes and he toppled to the ground. Yasmina had knocked him out with a stone from a sling.

'I didn't even know you had a sling,' said Jabir.

'My mother taught me to always have one last trick up my sleeve,' laughed Yasmina through gritted teeth. Her sling whirred above her head again, sounding like an angry locust descending on an ear of corn. She was intending to knock out Yusuf Said next but the landlord was swooping around too swiftly to make a good target. The stone got him on the cheek.

The landlord roared in pain but he was still able to fight. He lunged forward with his sword and this time it was Baki who screamed. Yusuf Said's curved sword had sliced through his thigh. He fell back against his camel who was snickering in fear.

'Jabir, Yasmina, here! Catch!' Wincing with pain, the guide reached into the saddlebag and a linen-bound parcel came flying through the air towards Jabir. The twelve horsemen!

'Quick, go,' shouted Baki. 'Stay on the path and you won't get lost.'

Both Jabir and Yasmina were back in their saddles within a moment. But so was Yusuf Said, blood pouring down his face.

'Ha! Ha!' He yanked the reins so hard, his camel cried out in pain. It thundered after Jabir and Yasmina, its hoofs digging deep into the sand. The desert shimmered in the heat, making it difficult to see.

'I think he's closing in on us,' cried Yasmina.

'Stay close to me,' Jabir called out. He sat up in the saddle, urging his camel to go faster. They came to a palm tree where Jabir stopped.

'We step off the path here.'

'Have you a plan?' said Yasmina.

'Follow me carefully,' grinned Jabir, 'and mind you don't accidentally step on any reeds lying on the ground.'

Behind them, Yusuf Said ranted at his horse. 'Hurry up, you stupid beast, or I'll cut you up for the roasting spit. Faster! Faster! They're getting away.'

But up ahead, Jabir and Yasmina had stopped. Jabir was holding out the parcel. 'Is this what you want, Yusuf?' he called. 'Come and get it. It's yours for the taking.'

'The boy is as foolish as his mother,' thought Yusuf Said. 'Why, I could chop off his hand as he stands there and the parcel will fall straight into my lap.'

He pulled on the reins to urge the camel on through the haze. Yasmina saw it rear forward. She saw Yusuf raise his curved sword. Then a moment later she heard a scream and the landlord vanished from sight.

'Where did he go?' she asked as Jabir.

'I lured him into one of those lion traps Baki warned us about.' Jabir grinned. 'I spotted it on our way to the wadi. I guess poor Yusuf will have to stay down there until someone rescues him, assuming he has enough water to survive. On the other hand, he might end up being a lion's dinner. It'll be the end of that snake in the sand, as my grandma called him. It's the camel I feel sorry for...'

CHAPTER FIFTEEN

Gold for the Horsemen

Shortly afterwards, Jabir and Yasmina reached Baghdad thirsty and covered from head to toe in itchy sand. Yasmina treated them to ice-cold sherbets from a stall on the edge of the souk. Jabir thought he'd never tasted anything as good in his entire life.

Safir shrieked with delight when he opened the front door. He called out to Abu Mahfouz who came flapping out of a temporary workshop he'd set up at the back of the house.

'We have the horsemen, Father,' said Yasmina.

'Well done! Well done!' cried Abu Mahfouz.

Jabir placed the linen-wrapped parcel on the table. 'Here they are, sir.'

The clockmaker opened it and stood the carvings one by one on the table. 'Magnificent! I can see where you get your talent from, Jabir.'

Jabir stared at the horses. Grouped together on the table as if advancing into battle, they were indeed impressive.

'Has the caliph extended the deadline?' Yasmina asked her father.

He shook his head. 'Sadly, no. The caravan going to Europe is leaving tomorrow morning. All the other gifts for Charlemagne have been brought to the caliph's palace already. We have to present the clock to the caliph at dawn.'

'Then we are doomed,' said Yasmina. 'We cannot possibly gild the twelve horsemen in that time.'

'Ah, but my friend Ali the gilder made a fantastic invention while you were gone,' said Abu Mahfouz. 'There is still hope. Safir will fetch him while you two clean yourselves up.'

Jabir could hardly contain his excitement as he did his ablutions. Then he offered a prayer of thanks. There seemed to be no end to Allah's generosity. But what was Ali's new invention? How could it help him gild all twelve horsemen in one night?

He heard a knock at the front door as he came down the stairs from the bathroom, smelling of luxurious sesame-oil soap. Ali had arrived. Jabir hurried into the temporary workshop where Yasmina was already helping the gilder unpack a wicker basket.

'Ah, here he is, our hero,' said Abu Mahfouz. 'Now, Ali, my friend, tell my daughter and Jabir all about your latest invention. They are dying to know how you will be able to gild the twelve horsemen by dawn tomorrow.'

'Necessity is the mother of invention,' replied Ali. 'When you came to see me, Abu, I knew I had to discover another process for gilding. So I went to the House of Wisdom and looked in a few books. I came up with a chemical formula to make liquid gold.'

'Make gold?' gasped Jabir.

'No one can make gold, no matter what the foolish Europeans think,' said Ali. 'You can only dig it out of the ground, or pan for it in rivers and streams. But you can mix gold dust with chemicals that will stick to any surface. It's much quicker to use than gold leaf. You just paint it on with a brush.'

He removed the lid off one of the jars from the wicker basket. The others came forward for a closer look. They could see a thick liquid in the pot. It was dark, like wild honey, but when Ali stirred it, it slowly began to glow.

Gently, the gilder dipped a brush into it and painted the beard on one of the horsemen.

'See how effective it is?' said Ali proudly.

'A truly marvellous invention,' agreed Abu Mahfouz. 'Keep the recipe a secret, Ali. It will make you even richer.'

'I have brought brushes for you all,' said Ali. 'If we work together, we should be ready by the third hour of the morning.'

* * *

The sky through the workshop window was still spangled with stars by the time Jabir put down his brush. All twelve horsemen were now gilded and they flashed in the lamplight.

Within the hour, the gold was dry and Abu Mahfouz fixed the horsemen on to the clock. He threw a piece of cloth over it, to protect it from dust, and Safir carried it out to the donkey cart. By the time the morning sun was touching the famous green dome on the caliph's palace, they were knocking at his door.

* * *

Jabir had often heard of the caliph's residence, known as the Golden Gate Palace. It was unlike any other palace in the world. The caliph did not want to hide away from his people. He wanted to be close to them, so he had allowed other houses to be built nearby.

The palace was surrounded by a freshwater canal and a curved walkway decorated with perfumed flowers. Only the caliph was allowed to ride around it on his horse. It was a place where he could relax and sort out his thoughts.

But there was no time to admire the exquisite building. They were ushered through one room after another, every hall grander than the one before. At last they came to a chamber with walls of polished marble. The grand vizier was waiting for them at a table.

'Is it completed?' he asked as Safir placed the clock on a round table.

'It will be in a minute,' said Abu Mahfouz. 'If I could have a beaker of water…'

The water was fetched and, under cover of the cloth, the clockmaker filled the hidden tank in the mechanism. 'We are ready,' he said. 'You may show it to the caliph.'

The vizier nodded and left the room. A few moments later he returned with a tall man in a white silk tunic and a golden coloured turban fixed at the front with a flashing diamond. His beard was flecked with white but he carried himself regally, like a prince.

Abu Mahfouz, Ali the gilder and Yasmina all bowed, and Jabir realised that this was Harun al-Rashid, the caliph of Baghdad and master of the city. In Ayat's fairy tales, rulers were always accompanied by dozens of courtiers and attendants but here was the most powerful man in the Muslim world, entering a room with only his trusted vizier for company. Jabir liked him at once and bowed with the others.

'Greetings, oh wise one,' he repeated after Abu Mahfouz.

The caliph was eager to inspect the clock. He tapped impatiently on the table as Abu Mahfouz carefully pulled back the cloth. His face lit up when he saw it. He walked slowly round the table, admiring it from every angle. 'Well done, Abu. Now tell me,' he said. 'How does this marvel work?'

The clockmaker had drawn new sketches to replace the ones lost in the fire. He spread them out on the table so the caliph could inspect them.

'Most ingenious,' said Harun al-Rashid. 'A miracle of science, really. But will it work?'

'We haven't had time to try it out,' confessed Abu. 'But I guess, with Allah's blessing…'

'… it's time to find out,' concluded the caliph.

Abu Mahfouz pulled a jewelled stopper to set the water mechanism in action. 'I will have to move it along with my fingers,' he explained. 'That way we can see what the clock does in a twelve-hour sequence.'

As Abu turned the hands, the bronze balls fell one by one through the trapdoor and hit the cymbal below. When each hour was announced, a horseman galloped out from behind a little wooden door to parade around the parapet. First there was one, then two, then three, till at the stroke of twelve, all the horsemen were leaping in a merry dance of flashing gold.

The caliph remained silent long after the horsemen had retreated into the tower and the little doors swung shut behind them. His eyes sparkled as he shook Abu's hand. 'Well done, all of you. I am more than amazed. Thank you, Abu

Mahfouz for designing and building the clock. Thank you, Yasmina al-Mahfouz for helping to build it and for designing the twelve horsemen. And thanks too to Ali, our famous gilder for covering them in gold.'

The caliph nodded at Jabir. 'And you, my friend…'

'He was responsible for carving the horsemen, oh wise one,' said Abu Mahfouz. 'We lost the originals in the fire but Jabir's extended family carved the new ones.' He indicated the horseman with the curved sword. 'This piece is his work.'

'Baghdad has produced many great artists,' said the caliph. 'But your work is truly exceptional. What is your full name?'

'Jabir ibn Abdel, the fisherman of the Tigris.'

'You have a rare talent, Jabir. Baghdad must nurture it and make sure it used for the glory of Allah. From now on, you shall be known as Jabir the master carver. This clock will enchant the Emperor Charlemagne and everyone in Europe who sees it. It will be a true testament of our Islamic culture and it will help foster ties between the two worlds.'

He clapped and servants rushed in to take away the clock. Outside, a caravan was waiting to transport the caliph's gifts to Europe. It would follow the same path through the desert that Yasmina and Jabir had taken. Then it would travel on to a bustling port from where the gifts would be carried by boat across the Mediterranean Sea to Europe.

'Come,' said the caliph. 'We must watch the gifts depart.'

They followed him to the front door where they were joined by a short man with straight hair swept under a round skull cap.

'A pleasant morning, Isaac,' said the caliph.

The man bowed in respect. 'To you too, oh great caliph. The eagerly awaited day has come.'

'Isaac is one of three emissaries that brought me greetings from the Holy Roman Emperor,' Harun al-Rashid explained to Jabir and the others. 'The other two have returned to Europe with our reply already but Isaac stayed behind to take the gifts.'

A large crowd had gathered outside the palace. Everyone in Baghdad had heard about the gifts the caliph was sending to Charlemagne and many had come to see them with their own eyes.

Jabir could feel the excitement in the air as musicians played hand drums and long reed horns known as zurnas. They produced a wailing sound that reminded Jabir of festivals and parties. A procession emerged from one of the palace outbuildings. First came a servant holding a golden dish and jug, both studded with jewels. He was followed by a second man carrying a carved horn of ivory, overflowing with fruit. Behind him marched other servants holding aloft huge jars of perfumed oils, a hand-carved chess set, brass candlesticks and a richly woven robe embroidered with the words 'There Is But One God'.

Next appeared three hefty fellows carrying the poles of a desert tent on their shoulders. The embroidered tent cloth was borne on a cart behind them. Last of all came the water clock, carefully placed on the lid of a cedar-wood box in which it would travel. The crowds gasped appreciatively as one gift after another was paraded around for them to inspect. Everything was so beautifully made, so richly decorated, the Holy Roman Emperor was sure to be impressed.

But there was one last gift still to join Isaac's caravan. A grey elephant with polished tusks was led out of the caliph's stables.

'His name is Abul Abbas,' said the caliph. 'He will cause a sensation in Europe where, to my knowledge, such wild animals have not been seen since Ancient Rome.' He turned to Isaac. 'Here are some dispatches for the Holy Roman Emperor. Guard them with your life. Tell him that I pray my gifts will please His Holiness and that they are seen as a token of our people's wish to co-exist happily with his own subjects. May Allah guide you safely to Aachen.'

Isaac put the messages carefully in a pouch and mounted a white horse. The crowd cheered as the caravan set off. The caliph put his arm round Jabir's shoulder.

'And now to less extravagant matters. Ones that nourish the soul and the mind. I am building a quiet reading room at the back of my palace,' he said. 'It'll be a place where I can indulge my love of poetry and stories. I intend to have the ceiling covered with gilded words from the Holy Book. Perhaps you can carve them for me.'

'I am sad to say that I do not know how to read or write,' confessed Jabir. 'I have not had the opportunity to learn.'

'Then my own tutors will teach you. You shall be able to read and write in no time. I shall teach you the skills of poetry myself.'

Jabir's chest swelled with pride as the caliph guided him along the corridors of the Golden Gate Palace. Just wait until he told his mother and sisters the good news. He was going to be working for the great Harun al-Rashid himself. And the vizier might go ahead and commission the chess set too. Jabir was now a respected carver, a *master* carver by the caliph's own decree. Even if Yusuf Said managed to get out of the lion pit alive, he wouldn't dare touch him now, a personal friend of Harun al-Rashid.

But most importantly, thought Jabir, his family would never go hungry again. He'd find a fine house in Baghdad for them to live in, outside the city walls at first, but soon, if his luck held and he worked really hard, they might afford a nice villa close to the caliph's palace. His sisters would make friends with Yasmina and they would all go and eat baklava and drink sherbet in the finest cookhouses in Baghdad.

The future looked rosy as Jabir stepped out into the sunshine. The muezzin was calling the faithful to prayer and he hurried to do his ablutions.

He had a lot to be thankful for.

Alhamdulillah!

Glossary

Abnay   my son

Alhamdulillah   a term meaning 'praise be to the Lord'

Bayt al-Hikma   meaning 'House of Wisdom', a famous library

Binti   one way of saying 'my daughter'

Divan   sofa

Dinar   a gold coin

Dirham   a silver coin

Djinn   a spirit, a genie

Dua   a prayer for help

Caliph   a ruler and a spiritual leader

Guitara   early version of a guitar

Imam   a religious teacher

Kamakh ahmar   a red cheese

Lakoum   a soft sweet, sometimes called 'Turkish Delight' in England

Marhaba   welcome or hello

Muezzin   the man who calls the faithful to prayer five times a day

Salat al-Isha   the last prayer of the day

Sayyid   master

Shukran   thank you

Souk   market

Ululated   made a howling sound with the mouth and tongue. People in many parts of the world do this to show joy or sadness.

Umi   my mother

Vizier   a minister at a ruler's court

Wadi   valley

Zurna   a long reed horn instrument, an ancestor of the modern oboe

HISTORICAL NOTE

This story is a work of fiction but it is set in a real city, in a glorious age that really happened.

BAGHDAD AND THE HOUSE OF WISDOM

Located between the rivers Tigris and Euphrates, Baghdad was the biggest city in the world for most of the Middle Ages. At one point nearly two million people lived there, and every household had access to fresh water, which was unheard of anywhere else at the time.

Baghdad was the capital of a Muslim empire, the Abbasid caliphate, and home to the famous

Caliph Harun Al-Rashid who features in our story. Under his rule, Baghdad became a world centre of learning and innovation. He built hospitals and established the Bayt Al-Hikma, the House of Wisdom, a private library that housed his collection of rare poetry books. In time this became a major educational academy, a sort of university, and housed the biggest collection of books in the world.

THE ISLAMIC GOLDEN AGE
8th to 13th century CE

The House of Wisdom was only one of many libraries and schools that flourished in Baghdad during a glorious period in history known as the Islamic Golden Age. In the early years of the eighth century, Harun Al-Rashid set up the Translation Movement. Muslim, Christian and Jewish translators flocked to Baghdad where they translated and preserved the writings of the ancient world, including works from Ancient Egypt, Greece, Persia, China and India.

Scholars, inventors, doctors, poets and engineers also came to Baghdad and the caliphate to study, work and share their discoveries. They made great advances in the fields of science, mathematics, medicine, architecture, poetry, music, engineering, philosophy, technology and astronomy.

We are enjoying the results of their hard work and inspiration to this very day. Famous people from this period include Ibn Sina (known as Avicenna in the West). A doctor and philosopher, he wrote a book called the Canon of Medicine. It helped doctors diagnose and treat hostile diseases like cancer. He is still known as the father of modern medicine.

The mathematician, astronomer and philosopher Hassan Ibn al-Haytham studied optics, showing people how an early form of camera worked, while a mathematician called Al-Khwarizmi invented algebra. This knowledge eventually spread to Europe and from there to the rest of the world.

A CLOCK FOR THE EMPEROR

The clock that Harun Al-Rashid sent to Charlemange was described in the emperor's official records of 807 CE. The author wrote 'It marked the twelve hours with balls of brass falling on a plate every hour, and also had twelve horsemen who appeared in turn at each hour.'

No one at the emperor's court could make out how it worked and many decided it was magic. It would be years before anyone in Europe could make a clock like it.

ACKNOWLEDGMENTS

As always, I have a lot of people to thank for help with this book: Hannah Rolls, Senior Commissioning Editor for Children's Educational Fiction and Poetry at Bloomsbury; my eagle-eyed editors Susila Baybars and Catherine Brereton without whom this story would be full of holes; Freya Hartas for her wonderful cover illustration that uncannily mirrors what I see in my mind's eye while I'm writing, and my tireless agent, Katy Loffman at Paper Lion Ltd.

Big thanks are also due to the many schoolchildren in Bradford and Leeds who encouraged me to write an adventure story with Muslim children as the main characters. This one is especially for you.

Also by SAVIOUR PIROTTA
ANCIENT GREEK MYSTERIES

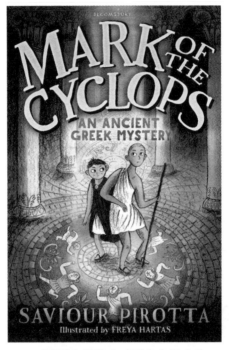

ISBN 978-1-4729-3414-7

Nico's new friend Thrax has a knack of figuring things out. When a valuable wedding vase is broken, his special skills come in useful. Join Nico and Thrax as they unravel the mystery and set up their very own crime-solving team, the Medusa League.

ANCIENT GREEK MYSTERIES

ISBN 978-1-4729-4016-2

Nico and Thrax are in the sacred city of Delphi while their master visits the temple there. But things are not as peaceful as they seem and a girl has gone missing. Can the boys find her and unravel the secret of the oracle?

ANCIENT GREEK MYSTERIES

ISBN 978-1-4729-4020-9

A valuable ring has been stolen and there's a mystery to be solved. But on the sea lurks a pirate who is also in pursuit of the ring and will stop at nothing to get it. Can Nico, Thrax and Fotini crack the clues, find the ring and escape from the pirates of Poseidon?

ANCIENT GREEK MYSTERIES

ISBN 978-1-4729-4025-4

Nico and Thrax are happy relaxing at home in Athens, but things get serious when they suspect a plot to assassinate a general, a plot by the mysterious Society of Centaurs. Can they and the rest of the Medusa League discover the identity of the society's leader and prevent the murder?